Carol Smith, formerly a leading London literary agent, now concentrates full time on her writing career. She is the author of ten highly successful novels, including *Family Reunion*, *Unfinished Business*, *Grandmother's Footsteps* and, most recently, *Without Warning*. For more information about Carol Smith visit her website at *www.carolsmithbooks.com*.

Praise for Carol Smith

Hidden Agenda
'Both a thriller – I was hooked by the very first page – and a gripping story about the power of female friendships – a winning combination!' Marika Cobbold

'A gripping and beautifully constructed story' Elizabeth Buchan

'Carol Smith has done it again, an unputdownable thriller with a twist . . . Smith holds the reader in her grasp from start to finish and gives us compelling psychological insights on the way' Julia Neuberger

Grandmother's Footsteps
'*Grandmother's Footsteps* . . . will keep you entertained, reading and guessing all the way to the end' *Crime Time*

'With its teasing insights into the mind of a serial killer, *Grandmother's Footsteps* keeps you guessing until the end' *Sainsbury's Magazine*

Unfinished Business
'If a pacy thriller is your thing, *Unfinished Business* will suit you to perfection . . . an addictive read' *Sunday Express*

'A thriller which certainly keeps you turning those pages . . . gripping right to the end' *Daily Mail*

Family Reunion
'A gripping read' *Family Circle*

'Full of action, twists and surprises, this intricate suspense story offers a fascinating new take on the nature of family ties' *Good Housekeeping*

Also by Carol Smith

CAROL SMITH

Fatal Attraction

sphere

SPHERE

First published in Great Britain in 2007 by Sphere
This paperback edition published in 2007 by Sphere
Reprinted 2007

A CIP catalogue record for this book
is available from the British Library

ISBN 978-0-7515-3798-7

Papers used by Sphere are natural, recyclable products made from
wood grown in sustainable forests and certified in accordance with
the rules of the Forest Stewardship Council.

Typeset in Berkeley Book by Palimpsest Book Production Limited,
Grangemouth, Stirlingshire
Printed and bound in Great Britain by Clays Ltd, St Ives plc
Paper supplied by Hellefoss AS, Norway

Sphere
An imprint of
Little, Brown Book Group
100 Victoria Embankment
London EC4Y 0DY

An Hachette Livre UK Company

www.littlebrown.co.uk

Acknowledgements

Tremendous thanks to my excellent backup team – my intrepid agent, Jonathan Lloyd; my enthusiastic and inspirational editor, Joanne Dickinson, and the rest of the Little, Brown team who are so much behind me. Thanks, too, to techno wizard Martin Dean of Smart Integration Limited, for showing me how to commit a perfect murder.

Part One

1

Rose was six the first time she killed, eighteen before she found love again. This time she knew it would be for keeps; nothing could take its place. Joe was playing in an Oxford bar when Rose dropped in with her best friend, Esther. It was instantaneous *coup de foudre*, though later even she didn't understand why. It was something about the sheer presence of the man. She wanted him on the spot.

With a cigarette glued to his lower lip, eyes half closed in rapt concentration, he played jazz piano with a quite extraordinary skill. Rose, very musical herself, responded to talent; this guy was good. But the session ended; he rose and stretched, dismissed the audience with a curt nod and made way for the disco. That summer the Police were topping the charts and the room filled now with Sting's rasping voice. The year was 1983, the start of the Michaelmas term.

The daughter of an architect, Rose had a scholarship to Magdalen College due to her quite outstanding performance in maths. That and her all round proficiency in music which had earned her additional points at the interview. They asked her to join the college choir, liking the fact that she also played the flute. With her self-assurance and keenness for study, she took as a challenge whatever she tried. So when she encountered Joe again she did not fumble her cue.

He had no idea who she was, of course, but she walked straight up and addressed him boldly.

'I heard you play. You are very good,' she said.

'And who are you?' His eyes were blank. *To comment on my playing* went unsaid. Doctoral students rarely mixed with freshers and Joe was on the final run towards getting his D.Phil in physics and maths. One of the brightest students of his year, destined, it was acknowledged, to go far.

'Rose Prescott,' she said, without a flicker. And took what she felt was her natural place at his side.

Rose had cracked maths by the age of two, helped by the numbers in the air that floated perpetually round her. Once she had tried to explain to her dad but realised from his blank incomprehension that she could never make him understand. She always got full marks in tests, the only thing that mattered.

'It's obvious really,' was all she could say when baffled teachers asked how she did it. From whence had come this astonishing skill in a child who could still barely read?

Whatever it was, it worked for Rose. She sailed through her education. The music, too, was an extra gift, not only the flute but her voice as well. A genetic throwback, perhaps, from the past had touched her with great distinction. For the first four years, as an only child, she was the focus of her parents' attention. They, aware of how bright she was, carefully monitored her mental growth and, when the flair for maths emerged, paid for a private tutor who was similarly dazzled. He had her tested; her IQ was huge.

'By the time she goes to school,' he said, 'she'll be eligible for Mensa.'

Her father, Matthew, was a private man who listened to music behind closed doors. Irascible, with a very short fuse, he needed his isolation. He was vastly proud of his gifted child and took her to concerts from an early age, though at home he preferred his solitude.

Oxford was everything Rose required to stretch her intellectually. She had chosen to study pure mathematics as a subject on its own. It was usual to combine it with something but, due to her startling precocity, the faculty allowed her to have her own way. A future

Nobel laureate, perhaps; an extra coup for the college that she was female. She studied hard, as she always had, at music as well as maths. The flute enabled her to unwind while the choir, when at last she got round to joining, provided a social life of sorts which took her away from her books. Music helped her to transcend; when she closed her eyes and relaxed her brain, she heard it in vivid colour.

'She's an odd child,' said Matthew, as ever slightly wary; what had occurred when she was six still gave him occasional nightmares. He was always intensely proud of her, even though she wasn't that easy to love. She seemed surrounded by a wall of glass that made it hard to touch her. Though he ached to hug her, he knew she would not respond.

'She gets it from you,' her mother sighed, with a deep-seated axe of her own to grind. 'She always was too clever by half. Is never likely to find herself a husband.'

Which showed how little she knew her daughter. Rose was already fatally fixated upon the only man she would ever love.

2

The Prescotts lived in Twickenham, the leafier, more upmarket part, in a house designed by Matthew himself, which had been greatly admired. Applauded too; it had won awards and was still the subject of much discussion. His name had been a byword for style before the world ever heard of Norman Foster. The rooms were spacious, with a Thirties' look, and the lawns ran down to the river. Rose and her much younger sister, Lily, had a tennis court and a croquet lawn. Lily would also have liked a canoe but her parents would not permit it. Something had happened, she didn't know what, but her mother always sat with her back to the water.

Bunty Prescott was a fading beauty with a waist the envy of women half her age. They had met in the early Swinging Sixties when she, white-booted and smoky-eyed, had run a boutique in the trendy King's

Road while Matthew was still a student. She had shared a house with a group of girls which was how they had met: he was somebody's brother. Rose had arrived in their second year after which they had largely run out of things to say. Bunty kept an immaculate home and fretted about the state of her tea cloths. Matthew worked longer and longer hours and had perfected the art of tuning her out.

'Mum,' said Rose, wearied by her constant fussing. 'Why don't you do something useful? Get a job.'

These days there was no shortage of money; Matthew kept them in affluent style. Anything Bunty wanted she could have. But her aspirations were shockingly low, at least in the eyes of her hypercritical daughter. Central heating, the latest cooker; a window cleaner on whom she could rely. She asked for little except affection which she got in limited supply.

A job? It was like a slap in the face. What had she done to deserve such a child who, since the day she was born, had been given the best? Rose was scornful and coolly dismissive. Think about women's rights, she said. Then she shrugged off her mother with an uncaring sigh and went back to studying Euclid.

When she wasn't wrestling with infinities or memorising a Bach chorale, Rose's preoccupation, till Joe, had been chess. Matthew, proud of her agile mind, had shown her the rudiments at six before turning in on himself for a while, leaving her to study it on her own. With her mother supine behind closed doors, Rose applied herself to the game, practising gambits and working out her own systems. She would happily sit for hours on end, stretching her mind to comprehend concepts that had baffled the world's greatest thinkers. An odd child indeed. The police had said that the time she had received the bravery medal.

Rose had always been self-possessed, preferring to do things by herself. She'd appeared unmoved by her parents' grief, though the doctor warned them there could be repercussions. She seemed to have taken so much in her stride. These days what had happened was no longer mentioned. When people asked if they'd like a son, Matthew and Bunty rapidly changed the subject.

'There are times she is almost too much for me,' Bunty confided to a close friend. 'I may be her mother but I haven't a clue what is going on in her head.'

Lucky, then, the advent of Lily who was all any mother could have wished for in a daughter. Petite and fair and nine years younger, she came at a time of such pronounced stress that Bunty had passingly thought of ending it all. Ingenuous and none too bright, all she had left was her shaky marriage, a daughter who clearly looked down on her and a house so clean it verged on an obsession. She developed migraines so severe that she had to spend hours in a darkened room, leaving her only child to fend for herself.

Rose hadn't cared, was self-sufficient, lost in her studies or playing the flute. When the unscheduled baby arrived she accepted it with her usual detachment. Matthew, however, was profoundly relieved and prayed it would have the desired effect. An incentive to pull herself together was just what Bunty needed. And Lily left nothing to be desired: she gurgled and wriggled and flashed those cute dimples, imploring anyone to pick her up and give her the necessary cuddle.

To be fair to Rose, she loved Lily too; there was nothing about her not to. She was cute and pretty, with a big beaming smile for everyone, regardless. Solemn Rose, in her navy gymslip, would treat the baby like an oversized doll, feed her when asked to, even give her a bath. Despite the image of that empty pushchair, Bunty implicitly trusted Rose. Her daughter was wise way beyond her years and had once shown remarkable courage.

While Rose had her mind set on higher things, Lily's main passions were trinkets and clothes. As sunny-natured as her mother, she had also inherited Bunty's looks, wide-mouthed with eyes of ethereal blue and a mass of curling fair hair. Bunty, restored to her radiant self, lavished expenditure on the child and had her hooked, from an early age, on the shopping expeditions that were her own lifeblood. Lily collected dolls and furry toys, wore ribbons and bracelets and neat white socks, the epitome of an out-of-date pre-Sixties child. Bunty allowed her to paint her nails and was always messing about with her hair. Though Matthew never noticed such things, Rose was disapproving.

'You're turning her into a Barbie doll. Don't be surprised when she's snatched by some dirty old pervert.'

Bunty, shocked, recoiled in distaste. 'Kindly mind your language,' she said.

'I am merely pointing out,' said Rose, always able to labour a point, 'that if you dress her like this at six, by eleven she will be jailbait.'

Rose, now fifteen, was in no way vain other than knowing she was mentally gifted. She was small and fine-boned, with her father's neat features and the narrow-eyed gaze of a watchful cat. From Matthew she'd also inherited her brains though not the talent that far outdistanced his. Matthew enjoyed his erudite daughter though longed for a son to ease the ache that Bunty would never discuss.

* * *

Although the sisters were poles apart, due to the age gap they rubbed along. By the time Rose was made head girl, Lily was still an adorable eight whose sole ambition was one day to have her own pony. She wanted to train as a vet, she declared, and live in the depths of the country.

No chance, thought Rose. She hadn't the brains, would be better off marrying young and raising kids. But she loved and tolerated the child, involved herself in bringing her up. In their different ways, they were both much loved and the family unit was tight and close, despite the occasional sadness glimpsed in the eyes of both Bunty and Matthew.

3

Being head girl in a single sex school suited Rose's compulsive nature. Since she had no brothers she rarely encountered boys. She was strict and bossy, though the third form adored her because of her innate chic and air of command. Her hair was glossy and neatly bobbed, her gymslip and blouse always flawlessly pressed. Her intellect and earnestness, in their eyes, added the more to her mystique. She was rarely late and finished her homework on time. *Should go far*, said her school reports. Matthew and Bunty were naturally pleased.

'Though I wish she had more of a social life,' sighed Bunty whenever they got her results. She didn't much fancy an egghead for a daughter.

'There'll be time enough for all that,' said Matthew, 'when she reaches the appropriate age.' With luck, she would get into Oxford, his own alma mater.

At home she helped Bunty clear the dishes, putting the cutlery neatly away, the forks all pointing in one direction, not dumped in a jumble as Lily always did it. She polished each glass until it shone then held it up to the light to detect any smears.

'You can leave that now and get back to your books.' Though Bunty was touched that Rose wanted to help, there was no necessity for it these days since they had a superlative cleaner. It was she, in fact, not the much-indulged girls, who kept things so spotless at home.

'I'm practically done. I'll just wipe down the table.' This drive for perfection was something Rose couldn't control. She had been that way from her earliest years, even sweeping up ashes from the grate. Disorder was something that actively upset her. The only way she could keep herself calm was by closing her eyes and counting.

Her bedroom was always immaculate, things in orderly rows, her schoolbooks filed alphabetically or else according to size. Her clothes were always put away, carefully colour-coded. She lined up her shoes with their toes pointing in, unlike Lily or even their mother, both of whom lived in a state of benign disarray. Her father found this neatness amusing but Bunty secretly worried about it; children were not supposed to be so controlled. She wondered how Rose would cope with sex, then guiltily shied away from the thought. In her day they'd taken such things in their stride. She wasn't so sure about Rose.

At school Rose was part of a tight little clique, all of them high achievers. Her best friend, Esther, was also trying for Oxford. Esther was flaccid and overweight. The two had palled up when they first met at school, on scholarships, both outstanding for their age. Rose shared with Esther her fondness for chess and they spent many lunch hours alone together, locked in a struggle of intellects. Their contemporaries considered them weird and, on the whole, kept their distance. Esther's distinguished father, Abe Newman, was a prominent trade union official; from him she got her persistence and lack of charm. She also got her obesity. Bunty regretted they were so close. She didn't want Esther's ungainliness rubbing off on her Rose.

'What *does* she look like?' She watched them play, heads together over Matthew's chessboard, Rose's hair always shiny and clean, Esther's a greasy mop.

'Leave them,' said Matthew. 'They are only fifteen. It is better for Rose to have a best friend than to spend all her time on her own.'

The role of head girl caused a huge change in Rose by helping develop her leadership skills. She enjoyed herself bossing the others around though she'd never consider trying it on with Esther. The two remained close throughout their schooldays though Esther chose to go to a different college.

Immediately Rose was settled in, the books on the shelves and her things stashed away, her main priority was to find a suitable accompanist for her flute. She had played since four and practised a lot and was now a very accomplished musician, another reason she'd been so taken with Joe. She was introduced to Hugo Penrose, a second year Balliol historian, who played the harpsichord almost at her level. Though in his shabby suit he was slightly nerdy, his performance on the keyboard really impressed her.

'Where did you study?'

'In London,' he said, shyly like an adolescent. 'I did a couple of years at the Royal College.'

Rose was impressed though did not let it show. There must be more to this callow youth than was immediately apparent.

She played some Mozart. He sang her praises. It seemed they were pretty well evenly matched.

'When can you do it?'

'Whenever you like.'

Another hurdle out of the way. Rose relaxed. Now that was sorted she could focus on the next goal.

They became a regular musical twosome, getting together every week or so. They quickly got on to the amateur circuit, giving recitals in village halls as well as occasional private soirees in front of the great and the good. Rose's parents heard them play and were taken by Hugo's diffident charm.

'I bet there's money there,' said Bunty, whose wealth detector was finely tuned. The instant she got home she would check him out.

Rose didn't do more than tolerate Hugo. A fine performer, he had nice manners but otherwise wasn't her type. Her type was Joe. Her mind was made up. Though she barely knew him, she'd always been single-minded.

'Give Hugo a chance,' said her hopeful mother.

'You have to be joking,' said Rose.

She badly needed to see Joe again but the only place she knew where to find him was at Rick's, where he seemed to be a regular fixture. Tuesdays and Fridays from nine p.m. on she was fairly certain of finding him playing, though it meant the risk of staying out after curfew. Normally a law-abiding student, Rose was prepared to take that risk, although usually he was surrounded by fans and showed no sign of remembering who she was. Nursing her single drink for the night, she would carefully work her way towards him, then speed off before they locked the college gates. He possessed a wide repertoire, and could play requests from across the board, but he mainly stuck with Thirties jazz which showed off his dazzling talent. Between sets he often improvised, eyes closed, entirely at one with the beat, scattering ash from the cigarette stuck in his mouth as he played.

'He should go on the stage professionally.' She wished he'd accompany her on her flute. Though not at all boastful, Rose was confident in those areas where she excelled.

'I think you'll find,' said Esther tartly, 'that physics would be a much safer bet.' Fond as she was of her closest friend, she deeply distrusted Joe's oily charm and didn't want to see Rose get hurt. She was only just out of school.

Rose, however, did not agree. 'I know we were made for each other,' she sighed. 'If only I could get to know him better.'

'Why not give the choir a chance?' Esther was very down to earth. The choir had always been part of the deal; Rose just hadn't tried it yet.

'I can't be bothered.'

'You never know. At least go once and suss it out. It makes better sense than mooning over a bloke who doesn't know you exist.' And was six years older and in his final year.

She did have a point. It could do no harm. She would try it once before blocking it out. So she turned up in chapel that Thursday night and came face to face with Joe.

'Hi,' she said, though he looked quite blank. He was even better close up than she'd thought. His eyes were appraising and toffee-coloured, his hair slightly burnished with gold. Her heart beat wildly. 'We've met,' she said. 'Rose Prescott from Magdalen. I heard you play.'

'The mathematician.'

She flushed with pleasure. He did remember after all. 'Are you in the choir?'

'I am,' he said. 'Why else do you think I'd be wasting time here?' He didn't smile, just looked grumpy and cross, turned his back and walked away.

Feeling foolish, Rose stood her ground, unable to think of smart repartee. He'd been coerced, a chorister said, because of his powerful voice. Which must be meant. Her spirits lifted. It was too much of a co-incidence. She was there too because they had drafted her in.

'I'll see you around,' she called but he didn't reply.

4

'Tell me about Joe Markovich.' Rose asked around but nobody knew. He was the cat who walked by itself, overtly gregarious yet a loner. She wondered about his provenance. Something about his looks smacked of the foreign though his accent was impeccably public school. He favoured jackets with elbow patches, worn corduroys and unironed shirts. His fingers were stained with nicotine and his hair was thick and often in need of a cut. When he laughed, which he seemed to do a lot, though in a slightly unpleasant way, she saw his teeth were perfect. But his wit was deadly as a viper's tongue and sharp as a razor blade. In fact, he hailed from the Newcastle docks, the progeny of an Estonian seaman who'd bequeathed him nothing beyond his name before sailing out of his life. Nothing tangible, that was. From somewhere must have come the prodigious talent.

Rose was hooked; it was like a drug just watching his fingers caress the keys. She had never felt anything like this before, was experiencing stirrings she found distinctly disturbing. She had never had crushes on film stars or singers or even the older girls at school. Had never been kissed or whistled at or been on even an innocent date. Despite her formidable intellect, emotionally she was a virgin. Now, though, she found it hard to sleep, went early to bed in order to dream about Joe. The buzz was that he was unattached though played the field voraciously. His doctorate would be in physics and maths though when he found time to study was hard to imagine. Apart from his two nights a week at Rick's Bar, he also bothered to come to choir practice.

Rose's compulsion developed fast. Though now he'd acknowledged he knew who she was, there were still occasions when he cruelly blanked her. Either he really was self-absorbed, his mind on a much higher elevation, or else, which seemed more likely, he was just boorishly rude. Whichever it was did not deter her. Infatuation had made her bold.

'One of these days I will get him,' she vowed to Esther, who merely sighed. In her opinion, it was high time Rose grew up.

Her chance came sooner than she had hoped. She was with a group in somebody's rooms when Joe walked in and casually greeted her. After a while they all moved on and ended up in his digs in town where, for the first time ever, he focused on her. The others slowly drifted away till only the two of them remained, earnestly talking, side by side on the floor.

'What do you mean, you hear things in colour?' At least he had taken in what she'd said. Which, in the few times they'd met, was a definite first.

'I just do,' said Rose, going on the defence, fearful of making a fool of herself. She was used to people considering her an oddball.

Joe, who till then had shown marginal interest, now tuned in fully to what she had said. 'Explain,' he asked again. 'I simply don't get it.'

'The colour. The music.' She was still very cautious, afraid he was just making fun of her.

'What kind of colour?' The grin had gone. He was intrigued; she was visibly getting upset.

'All kinds. I don't know. It depends on the sound. Different ones have different colours that meld together like . . .' She groped for the word.

'*Fantasia*?'

'I suppose so.'

'Tell me about the instruments.' Now he seemed really to want to know. 'What colour, for instance, are . . . trumpets?' He picked one at random.

'Yellow,' said Rose, without stopping to think.

'And saxophones?'

'Much paler. And, before you ask, the sound of a flute is a cool quiet green, the colour of bay leaves. Fresh ones, not the ones that are used in cooking.'

Joe simply stared. Was she having him on? It appeared not; her expression was grave. Till now she hadn't shown much of a sense of humour.

He was intrigued. 'And clarinets?'

'A livelier green, as in crème de menthe.'

'And drums?'

'Dark red with a brownish tinge.'

'And the harpsichord?' Had he heard about Hugo? She still hadn't figured him out.

'Tinkling white, like a waterfall.' Or ice cubes in tonic with a slice of fresh lime. Or the surf on a deserted beach in Cornwall.

'And my piano?' The grin was back.

'A kaleidoscope depending on what you play.' Now she was getting upset again, had broken out in a sweat.

Joe was more impressed than he showed. Her answers were so definite, he believed her. She sat there, serious as a child, hair dipping forward as she sipped her champagne. It was growing late but she desperately wanted to stay. Here they were at last in Joe's rooms, inches from what she had dreamt about. Let it be good, she silently prayed, hoping she'd know what to do when the moment came.

'Where do you get all that crazy stuff? I've never heard anything like it before.' What colour are your dreams? he thought. Or my lies?

Rose was nervous. She shifted position. 'It's a brain thing,' was all she could say.

Joe yawned and rapidly emptied his glass then stretched across and drained the bottle. His shoes were off. Now he unbuttoned his shirt. He looked so good she felt weak inside, had to use both hands to steady her glass.

'Come here,' he said and opened his arms.

She went to him willingly, like a child and every bit as trusting.

She woke abruptly with a throbbing head and a mouth as dry as an ashtray. Joe lay leadenly fast asleep. She quickly checked he was breathing. She studied his profile, relaxed in sleep, and a thrill swept through her. She had slept with him. Though she scarcely remembered a thing about it, their clothes lay tangled on the floor. She looked at the time: almost six o'clock. She would have to be off before the bursar caught her. She didn't know where the bathroom was but her bladder was sending urgent signals. She slithered silently from the bed and tiptoed off to explore.

The landlady's rooms lay along the hall. She was careful not to disturb her. Draped in Joe's shirt, which she'd picked off the floor, she found the right door and jumped under the shower which helped to clear her head. Rose was exultant. They were lovers at last. She couldn't believe it had happened so soon. She dried herself and towelled her hair then returned to find Joe still asleep.

There wasn't another sound in the house so she ventured down to the kitchen Joe shared and put on the kettle for tea. As she waited, she tidied up a bit, rinsed the glasses and put them away, carefully, side by side, two inches apart. She found a tray and two matching mugs, made the tea and took it upstairs.

When she opened the curtains he stirred and groaned then buried his face in the pillow.

'Go away,' he growled, three-quarters asleep.

'Tea,' said Rose gaily. 'Would you like toast? And how many sugars do you take? I've already added the milk.'

Joe raised his head and stared at her as if he had never seen her before.

'Who the devil are you?' he asked. 'Get out.'

5

All she could do was lurk and mope. Joe never so much as called her. She couldn't be sure he would even remember her name. But he must do; she had slept with him, had sacrificed her virginity and was now consumed by a burning need to see him and do it again. There was always chapel on Sunday, of course, but Rose didn't think she could wait that long. Whenever she wanted something, she wanted it now.

What was it like, Esther inquired as she made Rose coffee to calm her down. Privately she found the whole concept repulsive.

'Did it hurt?' she wanted to know, but Rose couldn't say. She had no idea. Even though she had bled a bit, the rest was a total blur. Sober, she was ashamed to admit she had acted like a slut.

'I love him so much.' She was almost in tears. 'What

if he doesn't know where I am?' The thought was appalling; she needed to get to him at once.

'I am sure he will figure it out,' said Esther, not adding *if he wants to, that is.* Joe's reputation was widely known She doubted Rose stood a chance.

Esther, though still very overweight, had adapted easily to Oxford life and found herself a niche group of peers with whom she had much in common. Not interested in the opposite sex, she was mainly concerned with getting a first. But hating to see Rose so distraught, she sacrificed most of Saturday to trawl the streets in search of the dratted man. Though certain it must all end in tears, she was too good a friend to spell that out while Rose was in such a state.

'Come,' she said when they'd walked enough. 'It's almost two. Let me buy you lunch.' Not used to exercise, her calves were aching.

'Wait,' said Rose, who would not give up. 'There's one more thing I need to do.' Leaving Esther standing there, she scurried into a florist.

Say it with flowers. It was obvious. She knew where he lived; it was not too late. If she wrote her phone number on the card he might even see her that night.

'You didn't?' said Esther, scandalised, when Rose returned with a confident smile. 'I can't believe you have so little pride. That's no way to catch a man.'

As if she'd know. Rose swept it aside and led the way into a pub.

Silence. Rose was mortified; could not believe her plan hadn't worked. On Sunday, after a sleepless night, she confronted Joe outside the chapel.

'Did you get my flowers?' She blocked his path, her manner suddenly menacing. Though fifty pounds below his weight, she was more than ready to take him on.

Joe looked blank. It was almost as though he didn't know who she was. Then: 'Roses from Rose,' with a mocking smile. 'Indeed I did. What a very sweet thought. Though you shouldn't have bothered.' He turned on his heel and wandered away to chat with someone else.

Rose couldn't sing; she was choked with rage. If she'd had a weapon, she'd have killed him there and then. Now, however, was not the time with the church bells ringing and in front of the choir. Rather than make a scene, she went straight home.

'I can't believe you could stoop so low.' Esther's disapproval was manifest. 'Can you still not see that the man's a louse?' Trust Esther to know how to twist the knife, though she did explain that was what best friends were for. 'You know I will always be there for you. He just isn't worth it,' she said.

*   *   *

Occasionally Hugo asked Rose out but found her unresponsive. He was nice enough but little more, a good musician who failed to turn her on. Tall and gangly, though with very nice eyes when he had the courage to look at her, he'd been steeped in the arts from an early age, educated to his fingertips with a pedigree to match.

'You could do a lot worse. And he does seem keen.' Esther had watched them perform together. Had seen his wistful glances when Rose wasn't looking.

'For goodness' sake,' said Rose with a weary sigh.

The fact was she wouldn't give up on Joe, was far too obsessed just to walk away; simply refused to accept he felt nothing for her. She decided to give him another chance but said not a word to Esther.

Joe was playing when Rose walked in, dramatically dressed in total black. It was late; she was breaking college rules but frantic to see him again. She had done what she could to look her best, was satisfied with the results. Now she was teaching herself to smoke so stood in the doorway and struck a pose where a spotlight instantly picked her out and Joe played a chorus of 'Lulu's Back in Town'. Rose relaxed as she watched him play, fingers gliding across the keys, then suddenly stiffened when he changed the mood and swung into 'Rhapsody in Blue'. It was aimed at her; she saw that from his grin.

'I dedicate that,' he said at the end, 'to the lady in black in the doorway. You'll not believe what she told me the other night.'

She tried to duck out but was just too late. Everyone had turned to stare at her.

'Bastard!' she hissed. They were laughing as she left.

6

In fury, Rose turned to Hugo instead. He still didn't know what was going on. Since it was almost the end of term, she invited him up to her rooms for a drink.

'When?' he asked, surprised and pleased.

'No time like the present,' she said. 'Around six.'

Hugo, with his impeccable manners, arrived at precisely seven minutes past, wearing what passed as his second best suit and bringing a gift-wrapped bottle. He made a clumsy attempt to kiss her but Rose deftly stepped aside. She wasn't remotely ready for that, not with Hugo.

'Sit,' she commanded, opening the wine and placing it in the fireplace to breathe.

She offered him crisps and little cheese whatnots, then fidgeted madly, unable to settle. He, embarrassed, examined the room, which conveyed a lot about Rose that he already knew. Curtains arranged into careful folds, cushions lined up in martial rows. Hardly a sign of real occupation; it looked more than anything like an impersonal show flat. When he raised his glass in a Christmas toast, she slipped a raffia coaster beneath it and gave him a linen napkin in case of crumbs. Hugo, whose family owned half of Hampshire, was secretly amused and touched. She tried so hard, her insecurity showed.

She put on some Bach and then closed her eyes which gave him the chance of a proper look. Up close her skin looked like porcelain and she hadn't a hair out of place. She was slightly built with a tiny waist and perfect ankles in dainty shoes. Her cashmere sweater was silver grey and picked up the shine from her earrings. He shifted his gaze when she opened her eyes, which were luminous and inscrutable as a cat's.

'What are your plans for Christmas?' he asked, anxiously seeking for something to say. He was strongly drawn to her which made him nervous.

He really is awfully drippy, thought Rose, although he did have beautiful hands; musician's fingers, sensitive and agile. Which instantly set her off thinking of Joe, whose own hands were workmanlike and strong, the thought of which set her pulses racing. She had fallen more than ever beneath his spell.

'Twickenham with the family,' she said, bitter because she had wanted to spend it with Joe.

'You'd be welcome at our place,' Hugo said. 'My sisters will be there and all their kids. My mother always keeps open house. It is usually very jolly.' Then, worried in case he had gone too far, he leapt to his feet and went to look at her books.

'Thanks,' said Rose, 'but I'm needed at home. They always make a big thing of it.' Her mother and sister went over the top which made her feel wholly de trop.

'Sorry,' he said. 'It was just a thought.' He had done it again, overstepped the mark. Rose was not at all easy to read. He could never work out what she was thinking.

'Let me top up your glass,' she said. 'After that I'm afraid you must go. I have things to do.'

My place Sunday. Cheese and wine, read the card Rose dropped through the door of Joe's digs when, three days later, she still hadn't heard and was on the edge of a breakdown. She couldn't believe he could act this way, after they'd been so intimate. In her grandmother's day, by now they'd have been engaged. All her anger had drained away. She wanted only to be with him. She closed her mind to what Esther had said. She knew, from the way he'd behaved, that deep down he loved her.

She also invited some of the choir, a few fellow students and Esther, of course, the stalwart chum she could scarcely function without. Not Hugo, though. He came on too keen. She would not risk his muddying her pitch.

She was in the grip of a manic fervour, wishing she'd thought of a party before. She booked a hairdo and bought a new dress with money advanced from her Christmas allowance. Bunty offered to pay for it all while Matthew also slipped her an extra something.

'I'm glad she's getting a social life.' Bunty was thrilled Rose was making friends though Matthew cared more that she pass her exams with honours.

The Magdalen Choir had been asked to sing at the carol concert at the Albert Hall the Sunday preceding Christmas. It was an honour, the choirmaster said, in the league of the Last Night of the Proms. But before Rose gave it a second thought, she had her party to give. She roped in Esther to pass things round, keen to put on a good show for Joe. Perhaps he might be persuaded to sing. Esther only hoped he wouldn't turn up.

'How about Hugo?'

'He's not on the list.'

'Pity. He's been a good friend to you.' He seemed a gentle and genuine guy who certainly didn't deserve such shabby treatment.

The party day dawned. Rose was full of nerves.

'Did you hear from Joe?'

'Not yet,' she said. 'But he's studying for his exams.'
Which had not kept him out of Rick's Bar last night.
Esther had secretly checked that out. He had stayed
late, till the early hours, and left with a girl on each
arm. She had done all she could; Rose was not a child.
At least she would be there as moral support if things
went disastrously wrong.

The choristers came straight from morning service,
remained in a group and were mousy and dull. They
drank very little though ate a lot. By half past two
they were gone. No sign yet of Joe who had not even
phoned. Rose, who had lost her cool detachment, was
suddenly looking tragic.

'Do you think I ought to pop over to check?'

'Don't even think about it,' said Esther, who couldn't
believe her friend could be such a loser. She was
smarter by far than the rest of her year but was now
behaving irrationally. The price of genius, Esther
supposed. Rose had led such a sheltered life and, in
many ways, still not grown up.

At four Rose finally gave up hope. Esther stayed on
to help clear up. 'Pull yourself together,' she said. 'There
are other fish in the sea.'

Sunday was the carol concert. A coach was laid on
for the Oxford group. Rose, however, would travel
from home since term by then would be over. Matthew

was pleased to act as chauffeur, might even stay on for the concert, in fact, if Rose could get him a ticket. Then Peter, the choirmaster, rang to say he'd be driving from home and could pick her up. Twickenham was on his way from Reading. He had one spare seat in his car.

So that was arranged. She took special care, when getting ready, to look her best. She was trembling now at the thought of encountering Joe. She intended to treat him with cool disdain to demonstrate how little she cared. Esther was right; the man was a total jerk.

Though that's not what she thought when the doorbell rang and there, on the step, stood Joe alone. Stubbing out his cigarette and looking apprehensive.

7

There had been a last minute change of plan. Peter's car had developed a fault so he'd hitched a seat on the coach instead and asked Joe to pick up Rose. She, caught totally off her guard, found herself almost unable to speak. Instead of the icy front she had planned, she seemed more of a gibbering wreck. Joe looked stunning, all spruced up in a sober suit with his hair slicked back. He gave her a calculating look but otherwise made no comment.

He followed her into the drawing room where Bunty and Lily were trimming the tree which was almost too big for the spacious room, practically touching the ceiling. Bunty was poised on a very tall ladder, fixing ornaments right at the top, while Lily, in one of her pretty frocks, jumped up and down in excitement. Matthew, as always, was sunk in the paper, unmindful of what was going on.

'Hello,' said Bunty, descending fast.

Joe introduced himself politely. Then: 'Whoa there, steady,' he said. 'Hang on to me.' He was there beside her in one swift move. 'We can't have you breaking your neck.' He reached for her hand.

The smile she flashed him lit up her face, knocking a full twenty years off her age. 'Thanks,' she said, handing Lily the scissors as Joe steadied her on the ladder.

Watching, Rose suffered a jealous flash. Why couldn't her mother act her age? The way she flirted with any male was positively indecent.

'Beautiful tree.' And beautiful house. He looked around with appreciation, admiring its clean architectural lines. 'I could almost believe,' he said, 'that it was by Lutyens.'

Matthew, inclined not to like Rose's friends, was startled by Joe's discerning eye, and agreeably flattered. He asked if he'd like a quick look round and, when Joe said yes, though they hadn't much time, shuffled his feet back into his slippers and took him on a tour.

Nice, thought Bunty approvingly when they returned. She liked his manners and the way he looked. Sophisticated and more self-possessed than other Oxford students she'd met. She didn't know he was six years older and in his final year. All of a sudden she understood why Rose, this evening, was looking so pretty though also apparently too wound up to speak.

'Look at me!' trilled Lily's voice, cutting across her mother's thoughts. 'I'm the Christmas Fairy!' She was balancing on the top rung of the ladder, arms outstretched and one foot extended. She had woven bright tinsel into her hair and was holding the scissors out like a wand. Even as they turned she began to wobble.

'Careful!' shrieked Bunty, losing her cool and leaping forward to stop her fall. But Joe was faster and got there first; was holding her safe in his arms.

'You stupid child.' Bunty almost lost it but broke instead into violent sobs. Her face was ashen and she was shaking. Joe looked on in surprise.

'It's OK,' he said. 'She isn't hurt. Just had a bit of a scare, I think.' Instead of immediately putting her down, he was gently stroking her back.

Lily, alarmed by parental wrath, twined her arms tightly round his neck and buried her face in his shoulder. 'Please,' she whispered in her little girl voice, 'don't be cross with me.'

Joe just laughed and ruffled her curls, transformed from cynic to avuncular ally. Time to leave. He nodded to Rose who was watching without a word.

They drove into town in Joe's MG without exchanging much conversation. Rose was nursing her rage at the way both mother and sister had behaved. It was ever thus: whatever she did they somehow contrived to upstage her. Even her father had joined in their act by taking Joe on a tour of the house, something, not being a braggart, he rarely did. Yet Joe had behaved like the perfect guest, admiring the house and, incidentally, her mother.

'She looks hardly old enough,' he had said, ' to have a daughter your age.'

They all said that. It made Rose sick. She couldn't decide who had acted worse, her flirtatious mother or the attention-seeking kid.

Speaking of which: 'What was that about?' He was curious about the unexplained fuss.

'Just over-protective.' As they'd always been. It was not a subject she cared to discuss, the family tragedy that had darkened her youth. Tonight was special; a date with Joe. She closed her mind to the past before it intruded.

The Albert Hall was ablaze with light, the crowds still filtering in. The rest of the choir were waiting in the foyer. Joe, in his usual uncaring way, forgot about Rose and just wandered off, the charm he had shown her parents now quite gone. It was always the same. Rose almost cried. She hoped he'd at least remember to drive her home.

The evening turned out to be a tour de force. Even

Rose, in her fragile state, was transported by the singing. The choirs, in their matching surplices, took it in turns to do their bit, then all came on stage together for the finale. The Christmas spirit was there in abundance. The audience screamed for encores.

Outside there was a nip in the air; the ground was already silvered with frost. Rose and Joe stood by his car as the Oxford-bound coach pulled away.

'Don't do anything we wouldn't do,' the lot of them shrieked in chorus.

Again they drove in virtual silence. Alone they seemed to have nothing to say. Rose had expected she'd have a meal with him but nothing was said about that.

'What are you doing for Christmas?' she asked, aware of the pathos in her voice. Damn. She sounded like Hugo but it was too late.

'I don't do Christmas,' was all Joe said. 'I'll probably stay in Oxford.'

'Then come to us.' The words were out before she had time to bite them back.

'Thanks,' he said. 'Maybe some other time.'

'Would you care to come in for a nightcap?' she asked as he pulled up in front of the house. She never had learnt how to leave things alone, as Esther had often observed.

'Thanks but no. I must get back.' He made no attempt to open her door or even switch off the engine.

'Thanks,' she said as she scrambled out.

'My pleasure.' And he was off. She heard his acceleration in the distance.

'Nice evening?' called Bunty who had waited up. 'I thought your young man might be coming in.' There were cold cuts on the kitchen table. She was now more formally dressed. 'I trust we will see him again,' she said having secretly fancied him herself.

Rose shook her head, too upset to speak, then bolted straight up to her room.

Make him love me, she implored the fates then buried her face in the pillow and wept. It seemed they were even further apart than before.

8

Rose's boyfriend he was dubbed by Lily, never the essence of tact. She wanted to know when he'd come again and if Rose intended to marry him. If so, she insisted on being bridesmaid. Idiot child; she certainly knew precisely which buttons to press.

'Stick to your Barbies and bunnies,' snarled Rose who, these days, seemed perpetually cross.

Covertly Bunty watched them both, concerned at the pain in poor Rose's eyes. The early stages of love could be searing, especially when, as she feared, it was not returned. By Rose's age she had known it all, including how to manipulate men. It was crucial never to lose the upper hand. Joe Markovich, with his sexy eyes, was far too worldly for her naïve daughter. Bunty recognised the type who wasn't safe in taxis.

'Why don't we pop into town,' she said, 'and get you an outfit for Boxing Day?' The neighbours always came in for drinks. Both daughters should look their best.

Rose declined. She would not be bribed and seemed reluctant to leave the house. She is waiting for him to ring, thought Bunty, aching to give her a hug. Which wouldn't have worked; she'd have pushed her away. Rose recoiled from physical contact unlike little Lily who could never get enough. Bunty could see Lily now, on the drive outside, practising on her roller skates, hair looped up into two cute bunches, frowning in concentration. She tapped on the window and Lily waved, her face alight with the fun of it all, then bravely let go of the hedge and staggered forward. What a great source of joy this late baby had been, arriving when Bunty had given up hope.

Although these days he was seldom mentioned, Simon was rarely out of her thoughts. They had been so alike, her two younger children: beaming, blond and benign. Twelve years had passed since his tragic death; by now he would have been almost fifteen. Sunny-natured like herself, he'd have had no problems when it came to sex. Not at all like his uptight sister, a spinster in the making. Lily was getting the hang of things now, was no longer clutching the hedge. Once she could balance, she'd be racing off. Bunty thanked God for this quiet enclave where children her age could safely play. Though it hadn't protected Simon, alas. She blinked and turned from the window.

Rose was still skulking close to the phone.

'Don't just hang around,' Bunty said, slightly more sharply than she meant. 'If you've nothing better to do with your time, pop up to the High Street and pick up some food.' At least it might help take her mind off that man who simply could not have cared less.

Rose was resigned to that fact herself. Today was already the 21st; Sunday would be Christmas. She wandered through the shopping mall, listlessly staring at tawdry displays, winking reindeer and laughing Santas that only increased her gloom. He'd not even bothered to send a card, surely the least she might have expected. She had sent hers off, with a friendly note, weeks ago. If he found himself with time on his hands, she had written, this was where she'd be.

And then, near a music shop, she was stopped by the sound of a tinkling piano, with a mellow voice and lively beat belting out Thirties jazz. Immediately drawn, Rose followed the sound and forced her way through the crowd inside until she found what she had been searching for. Fats Waller; she should have known. Ideal for Joe. She had it wrapped and rushed to the post. With luck, it might get there in time.

*   *   *

Esther came over on Christmas Eve, as she'd done every year since they first met at school, only now she drove her father's car instead of needing a lift. She had grown much more at ease with herself, was wearing makeup, had lost some weight and had finally tamed her wild frizz of hair by tying it back with wisps round her face that suited her very well. Rose was still in a feverish state, hysterically hoping to hear from Joe. This time, surely, he must respond unless it was stuck in the mail.

Common sense had deserted her. Esther, with a hardening heart, recognised the all too familiar symptoms.

'I'd phone him,' Rose wailed, 'if only I had his number.'

'For goodness' sake,' snapped Esther sharply. 'How can you let this guy ruin your life? He isn't worth it. You must see that by now.'

'I'm mad about him.'

'No you're not. It's just a delusion on your part that you really should have grown out of by now. Everyone knows he plays around and by that I don't just mean piano. He is turning you into a laughing stock. Get over it.'

'I can't explain. I've just known from the start that he is the one I am destined to be with.' She was close to tears. She gulped and blew her nose hard.

'Is it Rose's boyfriend you're talking about?' Lily had entered the room unobserved with a plate of brownies she'd helped to bake, fresh from the oven. 'She asked him here for Christmas,' she added, 'and he didn't even answer.'

'Go away, brat,' said Rose, enraged. The blasted child was always snooping.

'She cried,' said Lily as she skipped away. 'I heard her in her bedroom.'

'Is that true?' asked Esther, incredulously, not bearing to think Rose could stoop so low.

Rose nodded. 'You weren't supposed to know,' she admitted.

It was even worse than Esther had feared. She gave her friend a clumsy hug and repeated he wasn't worth it. His reputation in Oxford was bad for seducing women, then dumping them. This she had told Rose more than once but Rose still refused to listen.

'What did your mother think of him?' Bunty was expert in such matters. If anyone could see through Joe it would be her.

Rose sniffed again and wiped her eyes. 'She found him sexy,' she said.

9

Early in January Hugo phoned to say he had tickets for the Wigmore Hall. He sounded uneasy; Rose instantly softened towards him. It wasn't his fault; she knew he meant well. She would love to go to the concert, she said. She heard the relief in his voice; he would come and collect her.

No need, she said, they could meet in town. She had planned to look at the January sales. She hated the thought of her mother and Lily repeating their double act. They were like a pair of performing seals, forever grabbing the limelight.

'We'll come too,' said Bunty brightly, always up for a trip into town. 'I'll treat you both to lunch at Fortnum & Mason.'

'No,' said Rose firmly, her last word on the subject.

Hugo was not so bad after all; at least he had bothered to stay in touch and, since that single fumbled pass, had not come on to her again. She looked very good in her caramel coat and the long suede boots, a gift from her parents. Bunty watched her walk away. She hoped the trauma was over.

They met at five for an early supper at a pizza place in Marylebone Lane. Hugo looked older and even distinguished as he broadened up into his height. The meal was fun, and they laughed a lot; Rose was surprised by how much she'd missed him. He told her family anecdotes that showed him at his best. In all, there had been sixteen of them, with a grand piano and a nephew on drums. A proper Dickensian Christmas; very cosy. He was clearly very family-minded, was staying now in Richmond with an aunt.

'Which means I can drop you off,' he said, 'since it's hardly out of my way.'

Which was fine with Rose; she felt safe with him. Though she didn't invite him in.

Since they still had another two weeks to go before the start of the Hilary term, Hugo invited Rose to the British Museum. A medieval historian, he was very clued up in many subjects about which Rose knew nothing at all, having always focused on maths.

'I want to check out the coin collections for a paper I ought to have written by now.' He was highly motivated by his subject. Rose was intrigued; he seemed totally fired. 'I drop in here whenever I can. It's an education in itself.'

He was really cultured, though not pedantic, with the knack of bringing any subject to life. By noon, when Rose was starting to wilt, he suggested they call it a day and retire to the pub.

'We don't want to overdo it,' he said. 'Or else the magic wears off.'

He also took her to the V & A where a classical trio was performing live. They sat in the huge domed foyer and sipped mulled wine. Rose let her hair down and really relaxed, even managed a whole few hours without once thinking of Joe. They talked about music and Hugo's career. This was already his final year. He thought he would probably end up teaching in a prep school.

Esther was curious as well as relieved. From the little she'd seen, she'd approved of Hugo. And Rose was certainly looking much more relaxed. The easy friendship had obviously done her good. But Esther knew when to hold her tongue. One word in his favour and Rose might cool off which she felt would be a pity.

Back at Oxford for her second term, Rose threw herself avidly into her work. She'd continue to play the flute in public, liked Hugo enough not to let him down, but had more or less decided to pack in the choir. She had to cut back; there was too little time, and their public duets meant more to her than just being one among many. Esther approved of this wise decision, secretly hoped it might mean the end of Joe.

Her studies went well; she was making huge strides. The maths department was dazzled by her achievements. When Rose put her mind to anything, she went at it hammer and tongs. Her friendship with Hugo was slowly progressing. He made no secret of how he felt but kept his distance and left her to do the running. He had learnt his lesson: she wasn't easy. He would let things take their own course.

Lately Rose seemed more content, relaxed and in better shape. The twitchy tormented look had gone from her eyes. She smiled more, was even nicer to Lily, no longer batted her down all the time. She often spoke of Hugo and the music that they shared.

'Don't let the music take up too much time. Remember you've got exams to pass.' Matthew was quietly proud of his talented daughter.

'Don't worry,' said Rose. 'It's all under control. Maths is my life and music a hobby. If it weren't for Hugo, I might give it up, but I find his playing inspiring.'

Matthew and Bunty exchanged a look. He gave a knowing wink.

*   *   *

It was halfway through the Hilary term. Rose and Hugo were doing their stuff at a small exclusive reception at the Bodleian. Speeches were made by some notables; the Minister for Cultural Affairs was there. They'd been honoured with a half-hour spot before things broke for tea. Rose, in sage green, looking very demure, was in conversation with the minister himself when a voice she hadn't heard for a while hailed her from behind.

'Hi there, stranger. Where've you been hiding? I've been looking for you all over town.'

Rose stiffened and lost the thread of what she was saying.

'Sorry,' she mumbled and turned her back but the guest of honour had moved on, leaving her alone with her tormentor. Joe was looking good, no denying that, with that devilish smile and lascivious glint in his eyes.

'My dear,' he said, stooping to kiss her cheek. 'I've been wanting to thank you for your thoughtful gift.'

Her heart began to palpitate. She gripped the back of the nearest chair, then tried to move away but he grabbed her arm.

'Not so fast, young lady,' he said. 'We have some catching up to do. You don't come into the bar any more, nor have I seen you at choir.'

'I've been busy,' said Rose evasively. 'Studying hard for my degree. I've cut out things that aren't of real importance.'

'But you're playing today.'

'As a special favour. Hugo and I were coerced.'

'Good for you.' He squeezed her arm. 'That green exactly matches your eyes. Let's go and have a drink, little witch. You can catch me up on the goss.'

She looked around wildly, searching for Hugo who seemed to have disappeared.

'OK,' she said reluctantly. 'But just the one and then I must get back.'

10

'What on earth happened to you?' asked Hugo. 'I turned and you'd suddenly gone.'

'Sorry,' said Rose. 'I had an essay to write.'

'A shame. You missed the best part,' he said. 'They were rather hoping we'd play again.'

'Sorry,' she said again, sincerely contrite.

'When will I see you? We need to rehearse.' He knew not to try to pin her down.

'I don't really know,' she said. 'I'll check my diary.'

She felt so guilty, she couldn't face him; hoped she hadn't been seen with Joe. Was in even deeper than before and couldn't face hurting Hugo.

They had been to the Mitre, where Joe ordered drinks then led her to a secluded corner.

'You are looking really good,' he said. She melted. 'I liked the CD. Very well chosen, one of the all time greats.'

'I know,' she said. 'I have heard you sing some of his songs.'

'And will again, I hope,' he said, leaning over to stroke her hand. The eyes were shrewdly appraising her. 'How is your mother?' he asked.

And the cute kid sister? She inwardly groaned. The same old story; things didn't change.

'I have to go.' She picked up her bag and started to make an exit.

'Wait,' he said. He had hold of her wrist. 'Not so fast. Please. We need to talk. I think I haven't treated you very well.'

She stared at him coldly but didn't speak. If he only knew it, her heart was thumping. She prayed she wasn't going to blush or in some way let herself down.

'I'm not the easiest chap, I know. I've been told that often enough. You are going to have to give me a chance. I think we have some bridges to mend.'

The eyes beseeched but the smile was false. She felt he was laughing at her again. Hugo was ten times the man he was. Yet she stayed.

She started meeting him in the pub where the choir hung out after Thursday practice. Nobody asked where she'd been, she just melded in. Joe's manner towards her had fractionally altered: he greeted her warmly and bought her drinks, even occasionally draped his arm round her shoulders. He treated her mainly like one of the boys which, for now, was enough for her. He'd ignited her dreams again; she could only hope.

And so the rest of the term progressed with Rose at last able to concentrate. Now that the Joe thing seemed under control, she felt considerably less fraught. She applied herself doggedly to her work, was rewarded with excellent marks.

'Keep this up,' her tutor said, 'and you should get a starred first.'

She continued playing duets with Hugo; there was plenty of room in her life for both men. And she also frequented Rick's Bar again to be greeted like a buddy. What Joe did with the rest of his time was not her business; she tried not to mind. She knew she had Hugo as a fallback which helped make her feel more secure.

With Esther, however, she dropped the façade and talked about Joe incessantly. Her bottled-up feelings came flooding out; she seemed to be back to square one. Esther attempted to head her off but Rose was not in a mood to hear.

'I knew it would work out in the end. And that we'd end up together.'

The more included she felt at Oxford, the more she found she got out of it. Where maths was concerned she hadn't a problem, effortlessly sailing through every exam. She had such a phenomenal memory – one reason why she excelled at chess – she could do vast calculations in her head without recourse to a computer. Numerous times they had tested her, always with the same astounding results. When challenged to calculate in her head 37 to the power of 4 divided by 97, she came up with the answer straight away. There was no explaining this extraordinary gift, no known family antecedent. Matthew had always been very astute but in a more spatial way. He could look at a site and envisage a building but still required a calculator for the sums.

She joined the chess club, which was mostly men, then dropped out again when she found them so easy to beat. Joe played bridge and asked her along and she found herself part of a regular four who met on Sunday evenings at his digs. Again all male, they were physicists with the right sort of analytical brain to make them expert players. It became the high spot of her week; she liked not having female competition.

Slowly his friends resented her winning and after a while the invitations ceased. Joe explained that he worked now on Sundays.

'Typical men.' She virtually spat. 'Can't handle the fact that I am a far better player.'

*   *   *

The major social event of the year, looked forward to by most female students, was the Magdalen Commemoration Ball, shortly before the end of the summer term. Rose, who would normally not have cared, was as keen as the others to be invited and hoped that, now things were better with Joe, she might get to go with him. Her problem was Hugo, still dancing attendance and seemingly growing keener. Which was all very well but he must not stand in her way. In the end she took her courage in her hands and dropped in at Rick's to waylay Joe. They were, she felt, now sufficiently close for it not to seem presumptuous.

The bar, however, was in semi-darkness and the music playing was canned.

'No Joe?' she said.

The barman shrugged. 'He hasn't been in for a couple of nights. I tell you, the punters aren't pleased.'

Which was all the excuse Rose needed to confront him.

'Rose,' he said when he opened the door. 'How nice. What a pleasant surprise.'

He made no move to invite her in, just stood there awaiting an explanation. His hair was untidy; he needed a shave. She noticed his feet were bare.

'Are you ill?' she asked.

'Just working,' he said. 'I haven't got long to complete my thesis.'

For a moment she didn't know what to say and Joe wasn't helping at all. Behind him, she noticed, the bedroom door was ajar.

'My dad,' she lied, 'bought me tickets for the ball. I wondered if you would come as my date.'

'Alas, that night I am spoken for. They booked me months ago as the cabaret.'

And then, with a smile, he excused himself and closed the door in her face.

11

Hugo came through, as she'd hoped he might, and invited Rose to the ball himself which meant she wouldn't lose face. She consulted her mother on what to wear and Bunty suggested a trip into town. She was always up for some serious shopping, and then they'd have lunch in the Old Brompton Road which took her back to her single days and made her feel young again. Normally Rose disapproved of these jaunts, considering them an extravagance. Now, however, she was grateful for Bunty's support.

Lily wanted to tag along, even at nine she was mad about clothes, but Rose refused. She would only be a distraction.

'Tell her she can't, Mum,' she begged her mother who, this time, was on her side.

'You know you'll only get bored,' Bunty said and rang the mother of Lily's best friend to ask if she could go over there for the day. Nine years' difference could sometimes be tricky. Lily was still very much a child whereas Rose was an adult now.

She certainly looked it in the dresses she tried. She was small and neat and knew how to carry herself. With her straight dark bob and luminous eyes, she looked very striking in aquamarine silk, with a sweet-heart neckline and a tightly cinched waist that even her mother might covet.

'That's simply gorgeous.' Bunty was thrilled. 'With the right pair of shoes you'll be dynamite.' It was worth what it cost; the classic design should stand Rose in good stead for many occasions. Bunty said she could borrow her own mother's pearls. She was proud of her elegant daughter.

She also bought Lily a candy-striped dress with matching shoes and a hairband. She nearly always went over the top; the child was a joy to dress up.

'You spoil her, Mum.' Rose disapproved. Her baby sister was far too vain.

'You were nine once.'

'But I acted my age.' Rose had lived in dungarees until she went up to Oxford.

'But she doesn't have your advantages.' Which was what they almost always said. Because Rose was bright, she didn't need extra spoiling.

Today, however, she was feeling mellow and bought

Lily a bangle to go with the dress. It wasn't her fault Joe had let her down and, as baby sisters went, she had known worse.

Lily kept pestering Rose about Joe; when were they going to see him again?

'He caught me when I fell,' she smirked, as if that gave her proprietary rights. 'I think he's really cool.'

Bunty attempted to head her off, suspecting things weren't too good on that front. Hugo was taking Rose to the ball though Bunty sensed she would rather have gone with Joe. Where matters of the heart were concerned, her elder daughter was transparent.

'Shush,' she said and shook her head. But the tiresome child refused to back off.

'But what about Joe?' she persisted. 'I thought *he* was your boyfriend.'

'Joe is doing the cabaret,' Rose explained. 'Which is quite a coup in a town like Oxford.'

Just as well, thought Bunty shrewdly. He was much too worldly, definitely out of Rose's league. Attractive, indeed, with those sexy eyes but he had a strong whiff of decadence too. And, despite what he'd said about the house, Matthew had viewed him with similar caution.

'I wouldn't trust him an inch,' he had said. 'I know my own sex too well.'

*   *   *

The night of the ball was bright with stars by the time Hugo came to pick Rose up. He had cleaned his old banger and polished it, out of deference to his date. Rose, feeling great in her stunning new dress, had taken care with her preparations. The dress looked as though it were painted on. She had practised walking in the new high heels with a pile of books on her head. Her grandmother's pearls glowed against her skin. She had also borrowed her mother's mink jacket. Hugo was visibly stunned.

'Golly,' he said. 'You do look good.'

'Let's be off,' Rose said. She was shaking with nerves.

She held his arm as they walked to the car, then plonked herself in the back like a VIP. If Hugo minded, it didn't show. He found her insecurity touching. He was there for her but also prepared to wait.

The place was swarming, the men in white ties, many (not Hugo) in cutaway jackets, but the girls, on the whole, rather let them down in their juvenile party frocks. Rose felt like a star as she led the way in and saw the reactions all round.

First there was champagne on the terrace, after which they moved to the big marquee where a jazz quartet was belting out Sixties numbers. No sign yet of Joe, who was not billed till ten, though posters proclaimed him the main attraction. Before that there was the buffet to endure; Rose knew she would not be able to eat a thing. Surprisingly Hugo was a creditable dancer; it came from having sisters, he said. In his arms she felt like Ginger Rogers.

There came an importunate roll on the drums. The quartet stopped with a loud finale and Joe walked nonchalantly into the spotlight and bowed. In white tuxedo and cummerbund he looked every inch the professional player. He glanced around with those world-weary eyes as he stubbed out his cigarette. He took his seat at the grand piano, rolled in from the chapel at his request, flexed his fingers and shot back his cuffs then assailed them all with the most astounding sound.

He played for an hour without a break, to a background of stamping and wild applause, while the audience flung out requests which he always knew. Then he swung into 'Lulu's Back in Town' with a gracious nod that acknowledged Rose. She felt her heart might burst with joy as she wallowed in the glory.

By now he was mobbed by a gaggle of girls, one of them sticking her chest in his face, gazing at him lasciviously, practically down his throat.

'Who's that?' hissed Rose. She'd not seen her before.

'One of the bar staff,' somebody said. 'Her name is Shelley. I gather they are an item.'

12

They rode in silence all the way home, Rose no longer playing femme fatale. This time she sat up front and kicked off her shoes. Hugo, who'd got to know her moods, was also aware of when not to speak. By no means a fool, he knew the score; a girl like Rose, too good for that bastard, was also superior to him.

'Drop me here.' She put on her shoes. He opened his mouth then had second thoughts.

'Are you OK?'

She slammed the door in his face.

Back in her room, Rose fretted and paced. Checked her watch: it was almost two. The ball was over, the revellers gone. If she didn't move now, she might be too late. Her decision made, she stepped out of her clothes, smoothed down her hair and retouched her makeup. Then she picked up her mother's mink jacket and slid down the ivy.

*   *   *

Joe's digs, when she got there, looked fast asleep with only one light showing at the rear. She stood for a while by the privet hedge, trying to screw up her courage. He was hers, no one else's. There could be no dispute. And Rose always got what she set her heart on. Term would end in a couple of days after which they'd disperse for the rest of the summer. Joe would move on; she dared not take that risk. She had to do something to show him her feelings were real.

She braced herself for the ordeal ahead, drawing the jacket more closely around her and slipping on the shoes she had stuffed in the pockets. She was on a crazed adrenalin high, spiked by champagne and the mood of the night. There was no going back. She boldly rang the doorbell.

On the third or fourth ring Joe opened the door, his dress shirt wrongly buttoned. His hair was messed up and he looked half asleep. He was caught off guard when he saw who was there.

'Shush,' he said, 'or you'll wake the house. I am not allowed visitors after twelve.'

'We need to talk.' She pushed her way inside.

The door to his bedroom was firmly shut but the living room showed signs of occupation. Two empty glasses stood beside an empty champagne bottle. The ashtray was full of stubs, some with lipstick traces.

'Surely this will keep till morning.' He yawned and stretched, his eyes half closed.

'No,' she said, 'it most certainly won't. You might say it's a matter of life or death.' She allowed the fur jacket to slide to the floor and stood there, showing him all she'd got, a brazen smile on her face.

'Blimey,' said Joe, for once at a loss for words.

After a protracted silence while he stared at her, as though mesmerised, he asked her brusquely to put on her jacket and leave. 'I would drive you home,' he said, 'but I'm not alone.'

'But I love you,' she shrieked, tears bursting forth. 'You must know that. We are meant to be together.'

'I'm sorry.' Joe retreated towards the bedroom door which was now ajar.

'What the heck's going on out here?' asked a sleepy voice as the girl from the ball emerged from within and wound her arms possessively round his waist.

'I can't remember. Have you two met?' The insouciant smile was back on his face. Shelley was laughing too.

'If you'll wait a sec,' he said, his mood changing, 'I'll pick up my keys and drive you home. Can't have you running round starkers at this time of night.'

Rose, on the edge of craziness, grabbed the jacket and covered herself. With what vestige of dignity she had left, she made a rapid exit. He had treated her like dirt on his shoe and that was something she couldn't forgive.

Or forget.

13

Rose spent that summer in a state of despair that morphed by degrees into virulent rage. Joe had used her and publicly dumped her as Esther had warned her he might. Afraid of becoming a laughing stock, she went to ground and saw no one at all. Her reputation at Oxford was ruined; she wondered if it was too late to transfer. She had also been offered a place at Cambridge, as well as Imperial College. As soon as she could she fled home without saying goodbye.

When her mother inquired what was eating her, Rose would not be drawn. Something was obviously terribly wrong but she closed up like a clam. The dress had been a great success, was all she would say about the ball. She returned the jacket and her grandmother's pearls with barely a word of thanks. Bunty knew when not to interfere but hated to see her suffer so much.

It had to be something to do with Joe; that went without saying.

Hugo kept calling, he had lovely manners, but Rose wouldn't even speak to him. And, apart from Esther, who was on a kibbutz, she possessed no close friends. Not by nature gregarious, she viewed the world through jaundiced eyes. Acquaintances had to earn their way into her trust. Her fellow students were mostly men; pure mathematics attracted fewer women. Which suited her: she preferred them male, liked interchange devoid of social chitchat. Men respected her for her brain and aptitude for deciphering codes. She had soared through tests, remained top of her year, won awards and added to her distinction. Her future, once she had her degree, seemed comfortably assured.

'Do you know yet what you would like to do?' Matthew still hoped that she might join him. A brain like hers would sit well on his team and provide the continuity he had planned for. He'd established the practice for his son but either daughter would do. He was, at heart, a family man though only occasionally let it show. From him Rose had got her reserve as well as her talent. But architecture was not for her; she preferred the abstract world of maths to the mundane chore of solving practical problems. Her mind was fixed in a higher sphere, seduced by the beauty of the cosmos.

Lately, though, she'd become myopic. The only thing she thought about was revenge.

Bunty warned Lily to watch her step and not go bothering Rose too much. She was delicate and needed gentle treatment.

'She's always so grumpy,' Lily complained. She was almost ten and getting bumptious. 'She never wants to have fun any more. I can't see why she came home at all. I wish she'd stayed on in Oxford.'

Secretly Bunty sympathised, had been having similar thoughts. Nevertheless, she repeated her warning not to go riling Rose. Lily had eyes of cornflower blue and a smile of angelic innocence. The image of Bunty at that age; people found her impossible to resist. She was combing her rabbit on the kitchen step when Rose came down, having overslept.

'When will Joe be coming again?' Lily asked.

Bunty, frowning, headed her off. The child was doing what she'd been asked not to. The phone rang. It was Hugo.

'Tell him I'm out,' Rose hissed urgently but Bunty simply said Rose would call back.

'Do your own dirty work,' she said. 'I'm not telling lies for you.'

'If you marry Hugo,' said Lily brightly, 'does that mean that I can have Joe?'

71

'Out!' said Bunty, expelling both child and rabbit.

'Whatever it is, you can talk to me.' She boiled the kettle and warmed the pot. 'I hate to see you so upset. Is there anything I can do?'

Rose stared miserably into her bowl. There were tears in her eyes that she wiped away. Her hair needed washing; she had a spot on her chin.

'No one can help,' was all she said. 'I've gone and made a colossal fool of myself.'

With Esther away for the rest of the summer, connecting with her ethnic roots, there was nobody else in whom Rose could confide. Especially not her mother, though she meant well. So she started taking Hugo's calls, praying that word of her Joe fiasco had not yet leaked out in Oxford circles. Hugo seemed just relieved that nothing was wrong.

'You disappeared. I worried,' he said. 'I brought round bubbly to toast your results but you'd gone and no one knew why.'

'Sorry,' she said. 'I was overtired. Those last few days took it out of me.'

'As long as you're all right,' he said. 'I thought I might visit my aunt again. If you're not too busy, we might manage a couple of concerts.'

Typical Hugo; he didn't change. For the first time in days her spirits lifted.

'I'd like that,' she said and went to help with the lunch.

Hugo came up to London for two weeks, devoting the whole of his time to Rose. Bunty laughed; the aunt could scarcely have seen him. They took in a couple of exhibitions and went on an architectural walk. Hugo's interests were many and varied which made his company fun. Rose washed her hair and had it trimmed. Her mood improved; she smiled again. Having Hugo dancing attendance on her helped lance the pain in her heart.

'Now don't go leading him on,' said Bunty who had seen the way Hugo looked at Rose. He was far too nice to be messed about and she didn't trust her daughter. Rose simply shrugged; all they were was friends. Nothing harmful in that.

It was Hugo who broke the news about Joe, assuming, perhaps, that she knew already. He had got his doctorate and been snapped up for a very prestigious job. Los Alamos in New Mexico took only the cream of the top academics. Joe had already left for the States to join the nuclear team. Rose knew, of course, about the Oppenheimer bomb. The rest she swotted up on. She had always known he was very bright. The job he'd landed was a plum.

* * *

'Rose,' said Hugo, before going home to spend time with his parents before the new term. 'There is something I want to say to you . . .'

'Don't,' she said, covering his mouth with her hand. 'You mustn't risk spoiling our very special friendship.'

14

It seemed Rose had no cause for fear. Back in Oxford for the Michaelmas term all people did was congratulate her on her glittering results. She had Hugo with her as moral support and they started performing in public again. She was glad she no longer had to bother with choir.

Occasionally people asked about Joe. Rose replied enigmatically, liking it that she was still perceived as part of his life. Shelley, she heard, had quit her job in order to go on her travels again. Somewhere in the States it was thought. Rose tried not to let it hurt. At least she would not have to face her laughter again. The pain she had suffered gradually numbed to be replaced by an almost obsessive craving. She bought herself a Fats Waller album and played it endlessly late at night. Each time she heard it, she saw Joe's face with its sardonic smile.

There were photographs posted at the porter's lodge, professionally taken on the night of the ball; students were invited to order copies. Rose resisted as long as she could, hurrying past with averted eyes, but finally snapped just before they were taken down. And there he was, the star of the night, a cigarette jutting from his mouth, eyes half closed against the smoke, giving it all he'd got. She had to have one; she scribbled her name. And when, a week later, it dropped through her door, she hid it amongst her underwear to be taken out each night when she went to bed.

Whatever he'd done, she loved him still; was doomed to do so for the rest of her life.

With Joe not around, she could concentrate more so threw herself fervently into her work. If she couldn't have him, she'd at least get a first class degree. Her tutors were awed; she was smarter than them. They asked her to explain her calculations.

'How can you possibly do it so fast?'

'A knack,' she said with a shrug.

Less a knack than another aspect of the extraordinary gift she had. What she saw around her were clusters of figures that came in all colours and sizes. There were moments, like when she was falling asleep, that her mind filled suddenly with bright light and she was aware of swarms of numbers passing in front of her eyes. The experience was both beautiful and calming. In restless moments, as when thinking of Joe, she imagined herself in her numerical landscape. Doing so soothed her; she felt happy and safe. She was never lost: the prime numbers served as landmarks. No one knew, they would not understand, but it strengthened her inside.

Music, too, had the same effect. She knew where she was with a Bach cantata. Which helped her friendship with Hugo, too, though they'd never be closer than that. Increasingly she relied on him and he tolerated her quirky moods. In his eyes she could do little wrong so he always fought her corner.

Bunty kept on Rose's case, asking tactful questions without being too intrusive. Occasionally Hugo came to the house, once or twice even stayed overnight, but Bunty was sharp enough to detect they were nothing more than chums. It was all for the best; Rose was still very young with another whole year before graduation. Hugo would leave the following June, was already making plans. Travelling first, to broaden his mind; later, perhaps, trying his hand at teaching.

'You'll miss him when he moves on,' said Bunty.

'Perhaps,' said Rose, who wasn't remotely concerned.

Though for Joe she ached, missing him increasingly as the months rolled by and the pain of his betrayal slowly faded. She was eaten up by the thought of him, the single night they had spent together which, even though it remained a haze, was acquiring mythological status. From the time she woke till she fell asleep, progressively later the worse her obsession became, her consciousness was dominated by him. Though he never made contact, her dreams persisted until she began to embroider the truth. He was fine, she would say when people asked, though still extremely homesick.

Might she visit?

'I hope so,' she'd say. 'New Mexico, at this time of year, is magic.'

And where exactly was he? they'd ask.

She didn't know but made it up. In the mountains near Santa Fe, she glibly replied.

People sent messages which she passed on. So and so had been asking about him, she wrote. She sent her letters care of the lab, assuming they would get through to him. When she didn't hear, it only made her more keen. She filled her letters with snippets of news, sent newspaper cuttings and humorous cards; even started a diary. Things to tell him when he came home: details of who was dating whom, faculty gossip, even football scores. She talked to him constantly in her head, a witty intimate dialogue with jokes and comments on every aspect of her mundane life. Alone in the street, she would chuckle aloud, recalling some snippet she must remember to tell him.

When talking to strangers, as she did more and more, she would intimate they were very close, on occasion referring to him as her fiancé.

They would sympathise. 'It must be hard.' She was young to be separated from her partner.

Rose would smile bravely and silently nod. He wrote every day, she would tell them. She could hardly wait for their reunion. But when they asked when that might be, she had to admit she didn't know. Nor did she really know where he was since he'd never been in touch.

15

While Rose was finishing her degree, Lily was rapidly growing up. On the brink of her teens, she was starting to show a slightly subversive side. In place of the cute sunny-natured kid, a sulky nymphet was emerging who primped in front of the mirror for hours and cried if she found a spot. She lusted after the Pet Shop Boys and idolised Cliff Richard. As her hormones kicked in, so her body changed. She became a miniature of her mother, with the same flirtatious smile and honeyed curls.

'I warned you,' said Rose, when she acted up. 'You spoilt her and see how she's turning out.'

Bunty laughed. Rose was so uptight, especially now with her finals so near. If only she'd lighten up a bit. These days she seemed fuelled by perpetual anger.

'Leave her alone. She's still a child. Much as I was at that age. One minute playing with dolls, the next with boys.' Bunty had first started dating at twelve, younger even than Lily was now. It shocked her to see how fast her baby was maturing. Rose had never been through that stage, had switched from school-girl to serious swot whose sole recreations were playing chess and the flute. Lily showed none of her sister's precocity, preferring to hang out with her friends, swooning over teen magazines and pop stars. She'd not even passed the eleven plus, to her father's disappointment.

'I don't know what we will do with her. We'll probably just have to marry her off.' Not that she had any wifely skills. All Lily was good at was flirting and dressing up.

'You needn't worry,' said Bunty calmly. Lily was just like her younger self. 'She'll know what it is she wants the moment she sees it.'

Now that she was aware of boys, she squandered money on makeup and clothes, wheedling more from her over-indulgent mother. She was not supposed to stay out after nine, or ten if Matthew collected her, but had her own telephone in her room and spent most of her time on it, giggling.

She's a right little airhead, Rose thought sourly though she couldn't deny that Lily looked good. She'd mutated from childish gingham to sweaters and jeans. She had also taken to showering a lot which, since the two of them shared a bathroom, Rose found very annoying. Whenever she wanted to have a bath, Lily was in there first.

'Let her be,' said Bunty gently. 'You have advantages she has not.'

Which was how such arguments always seemed to end.

To no one's surprise, Rose got a first. Her parents gave her a Cartier watch and took her to Paris for lunch to celebrate.

'So now what?' asked Matthew. 'From this point on you may consider the world your oyster.'

Her prospects were dazzling: she had a whole choice of careers. The City, industry, education. Her tutors had begged her to stay on to do her Master's and D.Phil., but Rose had had enough of academia. There was virtually nothing she could not do except perhaps be an architect since she hadn't a spark of creative flair which, oddly, she bragged about. Matthew still hoped she might change her mind; she could take care of the business side and deal with negotiations.

Her mother, however, had other ideas. She sensed that the tension between the girls was largely due to Lily's hogging the limelight. Whereas once she had just been a charming child whom Rose could mother and boss around, she was now becoming a sexual rival. Which was natural, considering her age. The friction would pass once she was through adolescence.

'How would you like a gap year?' she asked. 'Or, if you prefer, a Grand Tour? Time off to see a bit of the world before making definite plans for your future? You don't have to worry. Your father will foot the bill.'

A light bulb went on in Rose's head. Why hadn't she thought of it for herself? A leisurely tour round Europe . . . or even the States. Apart from today, she'd been nowhere at all except once to Holland in spring to see the tulips.

'Talk to Esther and see what she thinks.' Even now they'd left school, they were still best friends. Level-headed and very well grounded, Esther would make the perfect travelling companion.

Esther, though, had other plans. Her summer in Israel had changed her. She now knew where her future lay: following in her father's tracks. The kibbutz had helped to focus her mind. She hadn't time to travel with Rose; she wanted to save the world.

Rose was amused. 'Just like that?' she said.

'The sooner I start, the better,' said Esther. Her name was down for a government job that her father was urging her to take. With him behind her, she should go far. He still had influence in the relevant circles.

Rose, however, had a different dream. She would cross the States on a Greyhound bus, heading straight for New Mexico in search of Joe.

16

She got off the bus in Albuquerque and took a cab to Los Alamos. A very long ride, over an hour, but she wanted to get there as fast as she could. And her father was covering expenses. Rose, with backpack and not much else, was travelling light as she always had. Neither extravagant nor overly fussy, she was doing it all on a shoestring.

Security at the nuclear lab was ultra heavy, which was no surprise, but finally she got through to someone who allowed her to have Joe's home address on hearing she was his girlfriend, passing through. He was off the premises at the time; it was after eleven on Saturday night. Rose, who had thought to keep the cab waiting, went back into town to flush him out.

The house was square and adobe built, not much to look at from outside but possessing a hidden court-yard behind high walls.

'Rose,' he said when he opened the door, dressed in shorts and a sweat-stained T-shirt. It was still very hot. 'What brings you to these parts?'

'I'm here to see you. Surprise!' she said, stretching up to peck his cheek as though they were friends, which technically wasn't true. 'Didn't you get my letters?' she asked.

'Yes,' he said but left it at that, seeming not at all pleased to see her, even after so long.

He led her inside – had no other choice, the streets being deserted at this time of night – and into a spacious living room that opened on to the courtyard. It was still so hot she could scarcely breathe, even at almost midnight.

'Can I get you anything?'

'Something cold.' She dropped her rucksack on the floor and unlaced her hiker's boots.

He brought her a Coke and a hunk of cheese. 'That's all I have in the house,' he said. 'I entertain very little.'

Joe seemed sober and more subdued. His pouchy eyes had lost their fire and his brow was permanently furrowed. His hair was shorter and flecked with grey. He looked considerably older.

Rose slumped with a sigh on the sofa and gulped down her drink.

'Rose,' said Joe, after a pause, seeming unable to

look at her straight. 'Tell me again why you're here. I don't understand.'

'I was passing through.' She mopped her face. 'And suddenly thought I would look you up, to catch up on old times.' She smiled at him brightly.

'You were passing through.' He looked at her now with the same shrewd gaze that still turned her on. Joe Markovich was a sexy man. Even her mother had thought so.

'Nobody passes through,' he said, taking her glass to replenish it. Rose sat gnawing the cheese, now faint with hunger.

'I did,' she said, 'and I sent you a card.' The last bit was a lie. She saw he knew it.

'Why are you here?'

'Oh, Joe,' she said. 'Surely you don't have to ask me that?' She dropped the act and fell to her knees at his feet.

He walked out through the courtyard doors and stood there, apparently lost in thought. 'I didn't answer your letters,' he said, 'because I didn't want to.' He turned to face her; his look was grave. 'We are two very different people now. You have got to get on with your life as I have with mine.'

'Why?' she said, scrambling to her feet, a shrill note of panic in her voice, but he put his hand on her shoulder and held her down.

'Don't,' he said. 'I want you to leave. We can't go into all that again. If you're honest, you know there was almost nothing between us.'

She tried to speak but he shook his head. 'Where are you staying? I'll drive you there.'

'Nowhere,' she said in a small scared voice. 'I just got off the bus.'

He showed her up to his one spare room, sparsely furnished and rarely used, and handed her towels and a bar of soap. 'Just for the night,' he said.

At seven thirty he tapped on her door. 'I have to go in to the lab,' he said. 'Help yourself to whatever you need. Do you know yet when you'll be leaving?'

'No,' said Rose, who had barely slept. 'I need to check with the Greyhound depot.' The sky was pink as the sun slowly rose. It was going to be another scorching day. 'Do you mind if I stay just a couple more nights?' She had come all this way and they still hadn't talked. She had so much in her heart to unload but he seemed not to want to listen.

'Two nights,' he said and closed the door. She heard his feet on the stairs.

She slept till noon, had a leisurely shower then wandered naked round the house, alert for the sound of his car. In the past two years she had lost more weight, so that now her ribcage was prominent and her pelvic girdle concave. She looked like a little bedraggled fledgling, fallen out of the nest.

She slipped on a T-shirt and brushed her teeth, then raided the fridge for a glass of juice which she carried out into the courtyard. With the sun now high the view was amazing, flat red desert as far as she could see with the looming mass of Mount Taylor in the distance. There were hummingbirds hovering round a sugar-feeder and the rattle of cicadas filled the air. Rose relaxed as she took it all in; she thought she could be very happy here. The heat was intense, though due to its dryness not unpleasant. She felt she would quickly adjust if she stayed on.

Joe phoned at six to say he'd be late, more likely checking that she was still there, and told her to make herself at home.

'I have,' she said. He didn't know how much.

She was in his study, going through files, reading his mail and checking his Filofax. She had started by searching for photographs and, finding none, was relieved. No obvious signs of a woman in his life. It was simple to pick out his inner circle: there were annotations beside some names, birthdays, names of partners, stuff like that. She also checked his appointments book to see which people he saw the most. It appeared these days he played tennis a lot with someone scrawled in as JP. No trace of Shelley which was a relief. She too, it would appear, was part of the past. Rose sat at his desk and carefully listed their details in her notebook.

By ten to eight, when Joe returned, Rose was dressed and the house was clean. She had shaken cushions and straightened rugs, scoured the kitchen from top to bottom and now had a casserole simmering on the stove. She'd found very little to stick in it; he had told the truth when he'd said there was nothing to eat. But by ransacking cupboards and emptying the fridge, she had managed to make a version of her mother's much-loved hotpot. She had also scratched through the thorny garden and found a couple of desert blooms which were now in a glass in the centre of the table.

He looked quite stunned when he saw what she'd done. She had even raided his laundry bag and a row of clean shirts was now outside, baking in the heat.

'You've transformed the place.' And in such little time.

'If I can borrow your car,' she said, 'I'll pop into town tomorrow and stock your freezer.'

'Rose . . .' he started, but she'd nipped away to pour him a cooling drink.

17

She gave him a list of things to buy; he didn't want her driving his car. As soon as he was out of sight she called the local liquor store and ordered delivery of two cases of wine. Rose had decided to entertain and didn't have very much time. Soon she would ring around his friends and make them promise they wouldn't tell. First, though, there was the house to fix. She was suddenly in her milieu.

She dusted the shelves, having moved the books, putting them back alphabetically or else, with the larger ones, according to size. Next she emptied the kitchen cabinets, swabbing down the insides with Lysol, and soaking the dishes to remove the thick layer of dust. The glasses she rinsed and left to drain; she scrubbed the plain pine table. The kitchen was cool, with a hard clay floor that she simply sluiced down with a mop. I am getting just like my mother, she thought. The fact was she was already worse. Bunty's standards were high but not compulsive.

Cleaning Joe's home was a labour of love. Rose worked hard with a song in her heart. If she put his house in perfect order and didn't intrude too much on his life, maybe he'd let her stay, at least for a while. She dusted throughout and swept the floors then ironed his shirts and hung them to air outside.

Phoning his friends was an easier chore. She settled herself at his desk with his phone and worked her way through the list she had made in her notebook. She was, she explained, a friend from Joe's past (she hinted at romance though did not overdo it), passing through on a flying visit and keen to meet his friends. She was bright and breezy and made them laugh. The vital thing was not to let him know. She wanted to thank them for being supportive of Joe.

'How sweet you are.' The one called Annette, wife of Joe's colleague Jean-Paul Gerard, loved the idea and offered to help with the food. 'I am sure I have heard Joe speak of you.' Her voice was warm with a hint of French that Rose found very attractive.

Rose doubted that but did not contradict her. Annette said she'd be there early and help dish out. That settled, she felt much more at ease and ran through the rest of the list without further qualms.

All would bring something and all would come. They swore not to breathe a word.

'What have you been up to?' Joe asked, appearing at dusk with his arms full of bags. He had brought back everything on her list, seeming not to suspect a thing, though looked with slight alarm at the gleaming kitchen.

'Earning my keep,' Rose said placidly, unpacking and putting the groceries away. 'Now if you'll go and change your shirt, I'll drop that one in the wash.'

He stared at her suspiciously then saw the ones on the line outside. 'Rose Prescott,' he said, with the hint of a smile. 'You take first prize for sheer nerve.'

He ripped off the shirt and tossed it to her, revealing a toned and well-muscled physique. Then, buttoning a fresh one, he opened a couple of beers.

They sat outside and watched the sky darken, the lights of the town pricked out on the desert like stars.

'I like it here. The air's so clear.' At this height, even the heat was bearable.

'So here we are again,' he said. 'How long has it been? Two years?'

'As long as that?' Two years, three months. And with each passing day she had craved him more. Though she now knew enough not to say a word, just silently thank her stars he'd allowed her to stay.

She told him about the first class degree at which

he showed little surprise. He casually asked what she wanted to do with her life. Rose didn't know; there was plenty of time. Her father had paid for this trip, she explained. She had got on a Greyhound bus in New York and simply followed her nose.

'You are brave to have done it alone,' he said. 'Few other women would have the balls.' Few men too; he'd been flown here Business Class.

They sat in silence and stared at the view, alone together for the first time in years. She hardly dared speak for fear of spoiling the moment. He talked a little about his work, the nuclear issues that were worldwide. It wasn't bombs he was working on but how to save the planet.

Rose snapped to attention. She was well informed and knew precisely what questions to ask to encourage him to drop his guard and possibly open up. This was something she'd always done. On a cerebral level they were very much in tune.

'Shall you stay here for ever?' she asked, hoping the answer would not be yes. Sitting quietly together like this was revitalising her dreams.

He didn't speak for quite a while. She even wondered if he had heard.

'Probably not,' he said at last. 'It depends on what else comes up.'

* * *

'Have you made any plans?' he asked next day.

'I'll stay till Thursday, if that's all right.' The party was fixed for Wednesday night, just twenty-four hours ahead.

'Up to you. There is no real rush.' Last night's discussion had mellowed him. She seemed to be playing it right at last by keeping it strictly low key. They had always been able to talk about things, provided she didn't move on to personal matters.

The principal thing in his life these days was his work. He left for the lab at a crazy hour, returning whenever it suited him. There was tennis, too, with his friend Jean-Paul. At Oxford he hadn't much bothered with sport but here, at Los Alamos, it was de rigueur.

'Tennis or golf. Sometimes both,' he explained. 'It's where the important decisions are made. And faculty members are poached by other departments.'

He enjoyed the game and was now very keen. It kept him fit and stopped him getting a paunch.

'Do you still play the piano?' Rose asked. It was there, in the corner, beneath a cloth.

'Not as much as I did,' he said. 'There never seems to be time. Though it helps me relax when I come home late from the lab.'

'Will you play for me? I'll be leaving soon.'

'Perhaps,' he said with a careless laugh. For a fleeting

second he looked like the Joe who had blown her mind in Rick's Bar.

'Tomorrow will be my final night so please try to get home early,' she begged. 'Sixish. I promise I'll cook you a special meal.'

He stretched across and took her hand. For one wild moment she thought he might kiss it. 'You know, Rose Prescott,' he said with a smile, 'you are not without your good points.'

Annette Gerard was a striking woman, French Canadian from Montreal with smooth dark hair and a truly beautiful smile. She came in carrying an earthenware dish which she handed to Rose before kissing her on both cheeks.

'It's so nice of you to be giving this party. The boys work so hard at the lab,' she said. Joe and Jean-Paul worked as a team. The research they did was hush-hush. 'I worry about the safety levels. They deal with radioactive stuff and have to wear astronauts' suits with special helmets.'

'Gruesome,' said Rose. Joe had not told her that. There was so much about his life here she didn't know. But she asked no questions; it paid more just to listen.

'They make a terrific team,' said Annette. 'As scientists and as tennis partners. I'm so happy for Jean-Paul that he has got Joe.'

She was treating Rose as a confidante, an important fixture in Joe's life. Rose fantasised she heard wedding bells; devoutly prayed that she did. Annette was clearly an ally to keep. She resolved to do her best to know her better.

She dug out some of the dishes she'd washed while Annette decanted her casserole, a spicy Mexican dish with beans and enchiladas.

'At first I found it too hot,' she said. 'We have nothing like it in Montreal. But gradually I adapted. People do.'

She was truly lovely; an instant friend. Rose felt happy and suddenly more secure.

Four married couples and two spare men; twelve including herself and Joe. Rose had excluded any spare women from her list.

'Hello. I'm Rose.' She wore her sole skirt and had managed to tart herself up a bit.

'What's the occasion?' somebody asked.

'An informal party,' she told him.

'What's the old dog been up to now?' Jean-Paul was dark with a close-trimmed beard. He'd arrived with Joe who was outside, parking the car.

Rose muttered something about their shared past, hinting at things that had never occurred. She noticed a few bewildered looks but nobody asked direct questions.

The front door opened.

'He's here,' someone said. 'Let's turn off the lights and shout Surprise!'

Rose had a passing flicker of doubt but by now it was too late.

'What precisely are you playing at?' Joe came into the kitchen and closed the door.

Rose, rinsing glasses, turned with an innocent smile. 'I wanted to meet your friends,' she said. 'Before I leave for London.'

'You had no right. Butt out,' he said. 'I am sick of your constant interfering. You never learn. You are at it again. Get the fuck out of my life.'

'But they seem so nice.'

'Which is not the point. The message you gave them is incorrect. You are not, never have been, part of my life. And, for certain, never will be. If you think that's going to change, you are deluded.'

'But I love you.'

'Rubbish. It's all in your head. It was never more than an ill-judged shag. First thing tomorrow you have to leave.'

'Please don't send me away,' she sobbed. 'Without you my life no longer has any meaning.'

18

From Albuquerque to Santa Fe Rose kept her head down and silently wept, wearing dark glasses to hide her shame from the world. He had done it again and mortified her, sending her off with a flea in her ear. Had not even given her time to say proper good-byes. Other passengers glanced her way but most had agendas of their own. Loners and transients mainly travel by bus. Joe had driven her to the depot and dropped her off with scarcely a word. It wasn't over, he said when she asked; it had never even begun. Forget it, he said, and get a life. He was not the marrying kind.

'Feeling sad?' a woman asked, aware of the clandestine sniffling.

Rose just nodded and groped for a tissue. She was leaving someone she loved, she explained. It usually took her this way. The woman crossed over to sit by her. She was large and homely with kind blue eyes. 'I'm a widow myself,' she said. She understood.

At Santa Fe Rose broke her journey to bathe her eyes in the ladies' restroom. He had tossed her aside like a worn-out shoe without even letting her have her say. Had told her she must forget him now. He had nothing to offer her, just as he hadn't at Oxford.

On the bus to Pueblo, two hours later, she made an effort to look alive. Immersed herself in a travel guide and pretended to scribble down notes. Her fellow travellers were native Americans who showed little interest in her. The road wound steeply up through the Rockies; she should be admiring the scenery. She had come all this way, five thousand miles, just for a slap in the face.

And then her outlook abruptly changed and something vital within her snapped. She saw with absolute clarity now what had happened. Joe had picked her out that first night at Rick's and led her on for his own amusement without a thought for her lack of sophistication. She cringed to recall how green she had been, the night they had ended up in bed and, later, her public shaming after the ball. She sat up sharply and closed the book, her eyes gleaming now like shards of steel. For too long she'd lived in a fool's paradise. Now she was going to fight back. She had just been awarded a first class degree by the best university in the world. Her future was assured; she could do as she liked. Joe might be bright but she was too. From this point on she would take control and, in the end, would triumph, she was determined.

At Pueblo a couple of tourists got on, heading for Colorado Springs, and fell into easy conversation with her. Both were teachers from the Midwest who had been to view their newest grandchild and were making it into a real vacation by travelling back through the Rockies. In their early fifties, they seemed well matched, smilingly at ease with each other. A couple truly in love, thought Rose, with apparently much in common.

They inquired where she was headed now.

'Denver, en route to London,' she said. She was going home to a brand new job. Her husband would follow later.

'And have you children?'

'Not yet,' she said. 'We've only been married a couple of years but have hopes.'

By Denver she'd had another mood swing, transported by her own fantasy. She swapped addresses with her new friends and also sent a card to Annette, apologising for leaving so abruptly. Something urgent had come up which meant her having to take the first flight.

She hoped they could meet up again in London soon.

19

Esther told her she'd been a fool, that leopards don't ever change their spots. 'Get on with your life and find a job. And forget that bastard,' she said.

'It isn't that easy,' wailed Rose, who was having a relapse.

'Easy or not, it has to be done.' Esther was not one for messing about. She was pleased with her government job which had great career prospects. She was with the Department of the Environment and already beginning to make her mark. Her father's reputation had helped, though she'd fundamentally got there on her own merits. She liked her colleagues as well as the work. It was one step closer to her ambition of helping to save the planet.

She told Rose that, with a first class degree, she could be fast-tracked by the Civil Service. The Department of Trade and Industry was in need of statisticians. Rose didn't care, a job was a job, but she filled in the forms and sent them off. Within a week she was offered a placement.

'The money's not great but the prospects are.' Matthew was very approving. He had long abandoned his dream of her joining his team.

'Nor will you have to pay rent,' said Bunty. The rail journey into town was direct. Having both daughters at home might prove tricky but Lily was almost through the difficult stage. With luck, Rose would soon have a life of her own and the childish bickering would cease.

Hugo was back and in touch again. After eighteen months he had tired of teaching and had joined a prestigious publishing house which could use his specialist knowledge. He had a flat in Red Lion Square, close to the British Museum.

'Why don't you move into town?' he suggested.

'Couldn't afford it,' said Rose.

Rose continued to seethe inside, unable to do as Esther urged and move on. Work occupied only part of her brain. Once she'd mastered the basics, the job was easy, allowing room for her simmering rage to fester into fury. She was like a volcano, on the surface calm but with a core of fire that often erupted. Her work-mates learnt to fear her short fuse and, as at school, backed off and kept their distance.

She thought of Joe incessantly, running an endless tape through her head. It hadn't been only in her mind: they'd had a distinct rapport. Those wise inscrutable old soul's eyes had singled her out that night in the bar. They had known each other in a previous life, she was certain. He just hadn't seen the truth of it yet. It might take time but she'd win in the end. She forgot entirely her resolution on the bus. Meanwhile the job was going well and soon she was promoted.

Directly above her in the chain of command was a plain-speaking northerner called Ann Cole. Fifty-something with cropped white hair, she held forth-right opinions on every subject, always delivered with heartfelt conviction though quite often wide of the mark. She took against Rose from the very start and, whenever possible, tried to put her down. Rose remained impervious to her jibes.

'Who does she think she is?' was Ann's regular moan.

Rose didn't care; she lived in a world of her own. The cerebral part of her job was automatic. Figures to her were as easy as breathing; beneath that level of consciousness, her mind moved on a more ruthless plane. If anyone flew in her path she would shoot them down.

And so it was with poor Ann Cole. Rose moved up the ladder in leaps and bounds and, in a couple of years, had displaced Ann by having her subtly side-lined. A feistier person might have quit but Ann stayed on like a thorn in her flesh, strident voice raised against her at every turn. Rose hardly noticed, was enjoying herself. She liked the kudos of running her own department.

Meanwhile, at home things had very much calmed. Lily was through the abrasive stage and back to her easygoing self, a bundle of laughter and charm. She was almost sixteen, would be leaving school but had no idea what she wanted to do. She talked on the phone for hours at a time and already had loads of admirers.

'It's a shame she isn't taller,' said Bunty. 'She'd make a beautiful model.'

The one thing Lily showed aptitude for was domestic science, which she learnt at school. She did more and more in the kitchen these days, especially liked baking cakes.

'If only someone would marry her,' sighed her father.

Rose worked long hours and came in late; she rarely sat down at the table with them. She was starting to find the journey home exhausting. After she'd eaten, she'd go to her room since she thought television a waste of time. She spent her evenings alone with a book or writing long letters to Joe. In her heart she had slowly forgiven him and was back again in fantasy mode. To start with, she only wrote them and never mailed them.

She also wrote to Annette Gerard, with whom she intended to stay in touch. She had liked her a lot and it meant distant contact with Joe. She hoped, if she made her letters amusing, news of her might filter through to him. Jean-Paul, after all, was Joe's colleague and best friend. Annette replied in short breezy notes, sending her snippets of local news, reiterating that her husband and Joe worked too hard.

Take a break and come over here. I would love to show you round, Rose wrote.

I wish, said Annette. *But there isn't much chance of that.*

Rose, emboldened, opened her heart and revealed to her new friend her feelings for Joe. *I believe we are right for each other,* she wrote, *and that some day he will come to see it. I feel so helpless not being nearer to him.*

Annette appeared to sympathise. *Never lose hope,* she replied. She made no mention of anyone else in Joe's life.

So Rose boldly mailed her next letter to Joe, then chewed her nails in anticipation. And when he didn't reply, she wrote again.

*　　*　　*

She kept his picture beside her bed as though he were suddenly back in her life. Bunty, tidying, studied it, the louche intelligent face. He wasn't handsome; he was more than that. The eyes compelled but it was the mouth that took her straight back, with a visceral shudder, to her own misspent youth. She saw why Rose was so deeply in thrall: he had a sexy and dangerous look. Those eyes could be those of a much more experienced man.

'Oh,' said Lily, when she came snooping, 'Rose's boyfriend is back in her life.'

'Leave it,' said Bunty. Joe Markovich was bad news.

'What's up with Rose?' asked Matthew mildly, having half overheard this exchange.

'Emotional stuff.'

'Good heavens,' he said, peering over his reading glasses. 'Rose with emotions? Whatever next! That's a first.' There were moments he felt he scarcely knew her. 'Who is the fellow? Someone we know? I'm assuming it *is* a bloke?'

'It's history now. Forget it,' said Bunty.

Matthew returned to his music and his paper.

20

Rose and Hugo continued to date though strictly in a platonic way. They went to concerts and sometimes museums; he was funny and kind and made very few demands. It helped fill in the gap in her life, when she wasn't working or dreaming of Joe who hadn't responded to any of her chatty letters. Annette, however, remained in touch with postcards and the occasional note. She worked as a microbiologist in the lab.

Without having to snoop, she kept Rose informed enough to keep her interest alive. He was over for dinner quite often, it seemed, and occasionally treated them to some honky-tonk.

He is awfully good. Annette was a fan. *I sometimes think he is wasted on science.* Jean-Paul was slightly ailing, she said. He had a perpetual cold.

*　　*　　*

Christmas came, with no word from Joe but a tinselly card in French from the Gerards. The Prescotts were all together at home with Lily, this time, doing much of the cooking. Next year she had her name down for catering school.

'You're a right little hausfrau,' mocked Rose, passing through. Lily had long been the more favoured child, at least in Rose's somewhat jaundiced perception.

'Not a lot wrong with that,' said Matthew, preferring his women traditionally inclined. 'Don't make fun of her. Let her learn. She may yet grow up to be a master chef.'

Rose merely sniffed. She was sick of Lily who seemed always to be at the centre of things. Her spots had gone, she was radiant again. The phone upstairs constantly rang.

'Be nice to her, she is still a child.' Bunty craved harmony in her home. Especially now, in the festive season, when memories best forgotten came flooding back. To lose a child had been catastrophic; she would cling very closely to the two she still had.

In the spring Rose received a note from Annette. The Gerards would be passing through London en route to Prague where Jean-Paul was presenting a scientific paper.

We are staying at the Savoy, it said, *and look forward to catching up.*

'Do you want to ask them here?' asked Bunty, dying to meet her daughter's friends.

'No,' said Rose. 'I'd sooner meet them in town.'

The meal was pleasant; they were both in fine form though Jean-Paul looked strained and had lost some weight. They spoiled her by booking a table in the Grill. Rose, having agonised over what to wear, was satisfied with the way she looked. Less is more was her mantra, and it suited her. They asked many questions about her job, laughed a lot and told scurrilous jokes. They were so in tune, Rose felt an insidious envy. If she and Joe ever got things together she would hope it might be this good.

Very little was said about Joe. He and Jean-Paul had their regular tennis but pressure at work continued to mount. Neither took much time off.

'How is he?' asked Rose.

'Much the same,' said Jean-Paul.

'Working too hard,' said Annette.

As they waved her off, Rose sank back in the cab. They were lovely people whom she felt she could count as real friends. Best of all, knowing them meant she still had a tenuous link to Joe's life.

Another Christmas and then another. The years merged seamlessly into one. At the DTI Rose was making a name for herself. She was in before hours and the last to leave. She kept her hair in a gleaming bob, wore tailored suits and crisp white shirts and her trademark high-heeled shoes. She still lived at home but found it a strain and was starting to think about moving out. She was earning more and hated the long journey home.

Lily, too, was growing up fast and nearing the end of her catering course. When people asked what she wanted to do, she surprised them by saying she thought she might run her own business.

'Doing what?' Rose was incredulous. There went Lily again, showing off.

'Wedding cakes,' she said. 'There is quite a demand.'

Not in Rose's circle, for sure; her friends were very career-orientated, but Lily had always liked to bake, had been making chocolate brownies since she was eight. She still expanded her doll collection but now was also a hit with the boys. They buzzed round the house as they never had while Rose was growing up.

Rose was reading a copy of *Cherwell* when her eye was caught by Joe's name. He was leaving Los Alamos and moving to the Massachusetts Institute of Technology, the finest in the world. There weren't many details about the job, except that it was a prestigious move. It listed his very impressive qualifications. By now he must be thirty-three; it was a full five years since they had last met. She paced the room in agitation; hating to think of him moving on without her knowing where he was or how she could stay in touch. She dropped a rapid note to Annette, letting her think she had heard from Joe but somehow managed to lose his new address.

'What business is it of yours?' groaned Esther, appalled that Rose could have so little pride. 'That part of your life is over. You should have moved on.'

Which was something Rose knew she could never do. She anxiously waited to hear from Annette and when her card dropped through the door, breathed a sigh of relief.

You can ask him yourself, was Annette's reply. *Tomorrow he leaves for Oxford.*

She tracked him down which wasn't too hard. There weren't many places he was likely to be. She had a short list of his Oxford friends and rang round them all in turn.

'Nice to hear from you,' one replied, assuming she must still be part of Joe's life. 'He's here till March, when he changes jobs. Back at his old address.'

The landlady, who'd never met Rose, didn't know who she was when she rang.

'Hang on a mo,' was all she said, 'and I'll get him.'

21

In the end it was Esther who saved the day, even though she still heartily disapproved. By pulling a few insider strings, she got a pair of opera tickets to die for.

'I don't know why I am doing this,' she said as she handed them over. 'Please don't come running to me when it all goes wrong.'

Rose was grateful. It was just what was needed to bait the hook she hoped might reel in Joe. The hottest performance to be seen in years, Pavarotti in a new production of *Tosca*, conducted by Domingo.

'Joe,' she had said. 'I would love to meet up before you move on to your brand new life.' She guessed he was unlikely to decline, he was such a serious opera buff. She was right.

Both parents were there when he came to the house and Lily was in the kitchen, baking. She'd just set up her wedding cake business and had a rush job on her hands. Rose, in the dress she had worn to the ball, classic and still a perfect fit, hovered nervously in the hall, checking out her appearance.

'Calm down,' said Bunty, surprising her there. 'Come and sit down and take some deep breaths. Don't let him see how het up you are. You'll only put him off.'

Her heart went out to her fragile daughter who had never learnt to relax with men. She feared for the outcome of this night which could end up breaking her heart.

When Joe arrived Bunty opened the door and showed him more warmth than she really felt. The danger warnings intensified when she saw how great he was looking. He had matured and the raddled look of a hardened roué was mellowed by a new and quite perceptible gravitas. He still wore his hair fairly long and slicked back but now it was elegantly barbered. The eyes were hooded and calculating but the sensuous mouth had not lost its appeal. As he took her hand and pressed it hard, retaining it just a fraction too long, Bunty felt like a skittish girl again.

'Joe, how lovely.'

He followed her in. Beneath the camel overcoat he wore a stylish suit. The move to MIT was a coup, another major step up the academic ladder.

He looked straight past her as she took his coat, to

Lily, standing in the kitchen doorway, wearing a chef's white overall, a smudge of sugar on her chin.

'Hi!' she said, embracing him. 'It's lovely to see you back at last.' Her face was flushed from the heat of the stove, she wore no makeup, her hair was a mess, yet still she looked adorable. Suddenly all grown up.

'You remember Lily?'

'Indeed I do. The fairy on top of the Christmas tree. The last time we met . . .'

'I was just a kid,' she said.

Joe reached out and caressed her cheek, wiped off the sugar and licked his finger. When Rose appeared without a sound and stood there, watching their inter-action, he didn't even bother to turn his head.

'Oh dear,' said Bunty, once they had left and Lily was back in the kitchen. 'I was sure no good could come of this. Poor Rose.'

The performance was all it was cracked up to be though Rose was too tense to concentrate. When, later, she asked Joe in for a drink, he surprised her by accepting. Bunty and Matthew had gone up to bed but Lily was still clearing up.

'Join us for a drink,' said Joe, draping himself in the kitchen doorway. 'You look as though you could use one.'

'In a minute,' said Lily. 'I'll just finish here.' The

sink was stacked with bowls she had used, her icing tools were scattered all over the table. She gave him the spoon to lick like a little boy. On a silver stand stood her masterpiece, a three-tiered wedding cake, just completed. She clearly did have talent.

Joe was completely taken aback. 'Did you do all this yourself?' he asked, indicating the bride and groom, both concocted from marzipan with a bridal veil of spun sugar.

'It's what I do for a living,' said Lily. 'I am not remotely clever like Rose.'

'Are you sure you're not too tired?' said Rose, interrupting. The brat was doing her thing again, stealing the limelight by monopolising her date.

'On reflection,' said Lily, getting the point, 'I guess you're right. I probably am.' She removed her apron and hung it up, then wished them a quick goodnight.

They sat in silence for ten long minutes till Joe said he ought to be moving on. Before he left, he pecked Rose quickly on the cheek.

'Thanks for everything,' he said. 'A memorable night which I won't forget.'

She didn't wait to see him off, just closed the door and hurried upstairs to hide her face and muffle her sobs in the pillow. When, next morning, she left for the office, Lily had not yet appeared.

And when, later, Joe telephoned and Bunty explained Rose was not yet home, he said it wasn't her he wanted but Lily.

Part Two

22

Lily and Joe were married in March, just eight weeks after their second meeting and days before he was due in the States to take up his new research post. Against her wish, Rose was maid of honour, in understated primrose silk. Bunty insisted she mustn't let Lily down.

There wouldn't be time for a honeymoon. 'I'll make up for that once we're there,' said Joe, still not quite able to trust his astonishing luck.

'Be sure to take care of my little girl.' Matthew was still not convinced it would work. It had happened so fast but Lily was now eighteen.

'I will, I swear.' Joe was clearly smitten. Throughout the wedding he couldn't stop gazing at her. Lily, who'd even made her own cake, wore a crinoline gown like a fairy princess, the way she had looked, he reminded her, that first fateful moment they'd met. The reception was deliberately low key: close family and a handful of friends; nobody from the bridegroom's side except the best man whom he'd privately earmarked for Rose. She, however, would have nothing of it, would not even wait for the bride's bouquet. She disappeared straight after the service though, sadly, was hardly missed.

Cambridge, Mass., was a whole different world, white clapboard houses with spacious lawns conveniently situated right on campus. Joe was now a full professor, briefed to propagate nuclear physics to a new generation of honours graduates, working for doctorates. Lily had almost nothing to do, the demand for wedding cakes here being sparse. They spent an idyllic five days on Cape Cod, where they spooned, held hands and made energetic love, both in the grip of an overwhelming passion.

Then, inevitably, it was back to real life. Joe threw himself avidly into his work, leaving his young, inexperienced bride to entertain herself. The faculty wives were all much older, most with absorbing careers of their own. Even the dinner party chitchat went mainly over her head.

'My poor little Lils sounds a trifle lonely. There's no one there remotely her age.' Bunty, still the obsessive mother, could not accept that her baby was now grown up.

Rose silently snarled and averted her face so that finally even her mother caught on and learnt to keep her mouth shut when Rose was around. So it had been with her long dead son. If only she'd learnt her lesson then, not to be quite so effusive.

Lily's first task was to sort out the house, which she found she rather enjoyed. Having always been the much younger of two, conceived, she suspected, to fill a gap, she had always been over-protected though very much loved. At home she was not allowed to use knives or even help with the kitchen chores, until she reached the age when she wanted to cook. Ginger-bread men and chocolate brownies were safe enough, under supervision, but the rest of it, the dangerous parts, had been seen to by Bunty and Rose. The catering college had opened her eyes and got her wanting her own domain. Now she could do as she liked without interference.

It was like being given a brand new dolls' house as well as the money to do it up. There wasn't even a limit on what she could spend. The previous tenants, both academics, had been elderly and childless. The living room had served as their work space, with fluorescent lighting and built-in shelves that entirely took away the period feel. Lily wanted it all ripped out and redone according to her mother's taste but Joe said he needed a study too as well as room for his books.

'Why not use one of the bedrooms?' said Lily. Four was more than they'd possibly need.

'Until we start a family,' said Joe. Which would also necessitate making room for a nanny.

The house was huge, with a morning room and screened-in porch as well as an open veranda. The kitchen badly needed renovation and that was where Lily decided to start. She spent many hours on the phone to her mother, discussing colours and specifications. Not too modern but elegant in the style of the one they had at home. She had never done anything like this before and had no idea where to start. Joe was more than happy to indulge her, though had to remind her that academics earn less than architects.

He was glad to see her enjoying herself and adapting gradually to his world. He was still enough besotted to indulge her. Rather than seeing them run up massive phone bills, he suggested Bunty should come and stay. He knew she was dying to inspect the house; he was more than happy to pay.

'Oh, darling,' said Bunty. 'What a lovely idea.' Matthew and Rose could cope for a week. 'As long as you're sure Joe won't think I'm butting in.'

Quite the reverse. 'It was his suggestion.' Lily was thrilled. She was missing her mother a lot.

* * *

Bunty still found Joe slightly unnerving, though now he was married he seemed more benign. His acid wit and lethal tongue no longer seemed quite so off-putting. He'd retained very little from his bachelor life beyond the imposing piano. They had rolled that into the drawing room and arranged a spotlight to show it off.

'Does he still play?' Bunty wanted to know. It had been an enchanting part of his whirlwind courtship.

'Now and then. Not often,' said Lily. These days he was mainly absorbed in his work.

'Is he good to you?'

'Oh, Mum,' she said. 'He spoils me rotten and gives me whatever I want.'

Bunty managed to keep off the subject of babies though longed for a grandchild to brag about. Having started early herself, she was still just on the right side of fifty. But she'd learnt enough not to interfere. Joe treated her with a grave politeness that made her feel she could not probe too much. She thought of Rose, still pining at home, aware of how bitterly hurt she had been. A child of Lily's would make her an aunt and might even help heal the rift between them. Rose had her own independent life, was doing exceedingly well. Though she'd never been the maternal type, a baby might reconcile them.

Mother and daughter had similar tastes and threw

themselves into the kitchen design. Joe would come home and find them together, side by side in the morning room, heads identical with thick corn-coloured hair, poring over catalogues and swatches.

'I trust you're not spending all my money.' He would smile benignly as he poured the drinks.

I think he really loves her, thought Bunty, relieved.

23

While Lily and Bunty were having a ball and recklessly throwing Joe's money around, Rose decided she needed a life-change too. She was too old still to be living at home. Even with Lily gone, it was time to move on. Matthew was sorry but understood, seeing the bitterness in her eyes. She tried to put a brave face on things but could not disguise the depth of her desolation.

'Whatever suits you, my love,' he said. He cared for them both, his two darling girls, was deeply saddened by what had occurred and wished he could make her feel better. He offered to subsidise Rose in a flat; he had, after all, paid for Lily's wedding. There were also people in the building trade who owed him considerable favours. But Rose, always fiercely independent, refused his generous suggestion. She was earning well and rising fast with nothing to stop her crashing through that glass ceiling. The last thing she needed now was her father's pity.

Hugo was still very much around. Rose took solace in his company. Sometimes, after a concert in town, she would stay overnight at his flat. Hugo, at thirty, had found himself and was doing well in his publishing job, part of a hot editorial team which was really making its mark. His Holborn flat was faded and comfy, with leather armchairs requisitioned from home and wall-to-wall books that made it musty and snug. He would rustle up basic meals in his kitchen and together they'd listen to the music they loved. Rose felt very relaxed with him and determined to find a similar place of her own.

Bunty returned with glowing reports of how the love-birds were settling down. The house was lovely and Joe a considerate husband. Any misgivings she might once have had were quite gone.

'Any signs of a baby yet?' Matthew was resigned to the marriage now, though missed his little girl and longed to see her.

'I need to get away,' said Rose, pouring out her heart to Hugo. 'All they can talk about is her. They're starting to drive me mad.'

Hugo had a dream of his own, that she might one day move in with him. Now, however, was not the time and Rose went on with her search. The flat she found on a Sunday trawl was in a Victorian red-brick block, just streets away from the DTI and close to the Catholic cathedral. It had two bedrooms, one minute, and a living room that caught the full morning sun. She knew at first sight that it was for her; had made an instant decision. She especially liked its proximity to work. With a little sprucing she could move in right away. Her father gave her the full deposit and Bunty chipped in with curtains and covers as well as a brand new bed.

'We are going to miss you, darling,' she said. 'But at least you won't be too far away. You can still come home at weekends and bring your washing.'

Rose didn't comment. Her mother meant well but all she wanted now was a separate life. Away from the painful daily reminders of how her baby sister had snatched her man.

She liked her job and was good at it. Working with figures helped keep her calm. To her they were almost like a first language in which she both thought and felt. They helped her deal with the tangle of her emotions. At work, though considered slightly strange, she was, on the whole, respected. She ran her department efficiently though went out of her way not to socialise. There were those who gossiped behind her back but mainly she was liked.

And now that she had a place of her own she could live a much more urban life, could walk to wherever she wanted in central London. As well as the evenings she spent with Hugo, she saw a lot more of Esther too, now sharing a flat with a colleague she knew from Oxford. Rose and Esther met every few weeks for supper, a film or some cultural event. Having been friends since their earliest days, they were still very much in tune. Esther, busy saving the universe, had begun a flirtation with politics, feeling she might be more effective with an official voice.

'Together,' she sometimes said to Rose, 'we could get this country back on its feet.' The Tories, under John Major, were palpably ailing.

Rose, though, was more of a back room girl with little ambition for overt power, preferring instead to operate with stealth.

At home, at night, in her silent flat, an endless dialogue ran in her head. Whenever her brain wasn't focused on work, she never ceased talking to Joe. With each breath she took, every move she made, he was never very far from her thoughts. To start with she'd been so angry and hurt, she had done all she could to block him out, but it hadn't worked, had only increased her depression. She hated him with a passion so fierce it was just as well they were far apart yet she ached for him too, even more now they had no contact. She had removed his photograph from its frame but not yet got round to destroying it. It still lay hidden among her things, to be taken out and looked at before she slept. She also kept the wedding pictures; bride and groom, herself and the best man.

She told Joe in her constant rambling the minutest details of her life, the concerts she went to with Hugo, her problems at work. She described the flat with its morning light and the arts and crafts fabric in mauve and green her mother had paid to have made into curtains and covers. She reminisced about things they had shared, the choir, Fats Waller, Rick's Oxford bar and that glorious gala performance of *Tosca* which had ended up wrecking her dreams. If only he hadn't come in that night on her invitation for one last drink, he might never have had the chance to fall for her sister. At which point she would usually weep. It hadn't been Lily he was meant to marry but her.

But even in paradise things go wrong. If Rose had still lived in Twickenham, she might have tuned in to that. Time passed and Lily kept calling home. She complained Joe was working far too hard, keeping ridiculous hours at the lab and paying her less attention.

'Surely,' said Bunty, 'it can't be that bad. It is just

an adjustment we all have to make once the honeymoon ends and life gets back to normal.'

The age gap between them was fifteen years. Whereas Joe was now at the height of his powers, Lily was still little more than a child, accustomed to constant attention.

'A baby might make all the difference,' sighed her mother.

'Or else some time apart,' said Matthew, who was badly missing his little girl.

He sent her a cheque to cover the fare and told her to come and stay as long as she liked.

24

She looked thinner when she stepped off the plane, though still quite outstandingly pretty, with her thick fair hair cut short which made her look older. The clothes she wore were stylish and chic; she had learnt to walk like a model. Both her parents were there to meet her and she ran to hug them like the child that, at heart, she still was. Bunty sensed a feeling of faint desperation.

'Hello, poppet.'

Lily clung to her then moved to embrace her father too. He patted her clumsily on the back, averting his face to conceal spontaneous tears.

'Where's Rose?' she asked when they reached the house.

'Moved out,' said Bunty who knew she had been told. 'She found the daily journey too much. Bought a flat close to work.'

Typical Lily who never listened, self-absorbed as she always was. Partly their fault for spoiling her but now she was grown up and a married woman.

'How's Joe?'

'He's fine. Sends you both his love.'

'Doesn't he mind us snatching you away?'

'I have no doubt he can manage without me,' she said.

She shot upstairs to change her clothes and came down looking like a child again in scruffy jeans with a rip in the knee and a tight-fitting blue and white T-shirt.

'That's more like it,' said Matthew gruffly. 'I've got my little girl back.'

'How do you think she seems?' he asked when Lily, exhausted, had gone to bed.

'I am not quite sure,' said Bunty, thoughtful. 'I'd say she has things on her mind.'

It wasn't just Joe, it was Cambridge too. She found it lonely when he was at work which, lately, seemed to be most of his waking hours.

'There must be something you could do. Party planning or private catering.' She had, after all, the qualifications and it was a university town.

Lily said no, at least not where they lived. Joe's friends were stuffy and wouldn't approve of her earning her living that way. They were most of them older by a good twenty years, Joe being one of the youngest professors on campus.

So how about the wives, Bunty asked. Couldn't she try to make friends with them?

'The ones my age all have kids,' Lily said. 'I feel like an outsider.'

So that's what it was: she was too much alone. What she mainly lacked was a kindred spirit. She needed someone with similar tastes for shopping sprees and occasional lunches, someone to go to the pictures with or the gym.

Joe had also stopped playing the piano at night. Directly he'd eaten he went upstairs and immersed himself in his books.

'Just like your dad.' Bunty knew how it felt; without her friends she'd be similarly lost. The problem with these cerebral men was that they shut you out.

She was only home a couple of weeks. Bunty asked Rose to come for Sunday lunch. Rose said no, she hated Lily, did not intend to see her again. Would never forgive what she had done and that was the end of it.

'But, after us, she's your closest kin.' Bunty was keen they should make it up. 'Once we have gone, she's all the family you'll have.'

'Why should I care?' She would never forgive; it was not in her nature to do so.

'Why not bring Hugo too?' said Bunty, trying another crafty tack. They were good together; he made Rose more relaxed. Hugo, at thirty, had really filled out and become a very presentable man. He wore his pre-Raphaelite curls quite long and still had those gorgeous lashes. He affected cravats and velvet jackets and looked every inch the aesthete he was but also had the unusual knack of helping Rose loosen up. Bunty still had hopes they might marry; he was said to be very comfortably off and must have some sort of feeling for Rose or he wouldn't still be around.

'Just this once,' she begged. 'For me.' Hugo hadn't been out to the house for a while. 'You don't want Lily to think she's won and that you still care about Joe.'

Which worked, as Bunty had known it would. Rose was angry but also proud. She said she'd come but only if Hugo was free.

As indeed he was. He leapt at the chance to spend more time in the Prescott home. He liked both parents and knew he would get a good meal. He hadn't seen Lily for many years, remembered her just as a ravishing child with her mother's sunny nature and radiant smile. When they reached the house and she opened the door he was, for a second, gobsmacked. The child was now a beautiful woman with a stunning figure and flawless skin, a cloud of fair hair and a pouting, bee-stung mouth.

'Hugo!' She threw herself into his arms as though he were her dearest friend. He had never had such a welcome from Rose, he reflected.

Lily then also hugged her sister. Rose, though rigid, did not shake her off. Bunty silently sighed with relief. It was time that they reached a truce.

The garden was looking at its best. It was April and unseasonably warm. They carried their drinks to the water's edge except for Bunty who stayed behind in the kitchen. Lily perched on the garden table, flirting madly and swinging her legs. She knew she looked good and liked nothing more than to be the focus of male attention. Even Hugo would serve; she was showing off. She prattled on about MIT; Joe, she explained, had been too busy to come.

'Poor baby, he works so hard,' she said. 'I feel guilty at leaving him on his own. But I needed a break and have shopping to do. He spoils me rotten, is such a darling man.'

Rose wandered off. Hugo watched her go. He could tell from her stance she was gritting her teeth. How well he knew her. If only she'd learn to relax. Lily, impervious to anyone else, babbled on like the child she still was. Joe, she said, was an absolute saint. The very best husband a girl could have. She wasn't sure she deserved him.

'Shut up!' Rose suddenly turned and screeched, her face chalk-white and her eyes ablaze. 'Can't you bloody well talk about anything else?'

Lily raised innocent eyes to her, startled by this explosion of wrath. Poor old Rose was so uptight and, furthermore, losing her looks. She also seemed to have lost what humour she'd had.

'It's just as well,' she said with a laugh, 'that you and Joe didn't end up together. At least I bring out his lighter side. Together you must have been murder.'

Somewhere offstage a telephone rang. Bunty appeared at the kitchen door.

'Lily,' she called. 'It's Joe for you. Better hurry.'

25

Joe had called with excellent news, at least from his point of view, Lily said. His friend, Jean-Paul from Los Alamos, was joining him at MIT, along with his microbiologist wife Annette.

'Aren't they the people you met?' inquired Bunty, once they were all sitting down to lunch. Rose nodded curtly. She seemed unable to speak.

'You really liked them, didn't you, dear? I think you said you were still in touch. Nice for Lily to get to know your friends.'

Lily, however, failed to respond. She hated it when the spotlight wasn't on her.

'Give me a break,' was all she said, flashing that smile at the mesmerised Hugo. 'They are bound to be too old for me. Fuddy-duddies like the rest of my husband's set.'

'Oh, come now,' said Bunty while Matthew carved. 'You should make some sort of effort for them. They were kind to Rose. Remember she is your sister.'

Rose, almost choking, threw down her napkin and stormed from the room in a terrible rage. It wasn't fair; she had had enough, was on the brink of provoking a serious fight.

Tactfully, Hugo checked the time. Soon, he suggested, they should be off. Sunday traffic along the river could often be very heavy.

Rose, in the privacy of her room, left unaltered since the day she moved out, took great gulps of air and tried to calm down. They were her friends, not Lily's; it was happening again, Lily encroaching on her territory. She hurled her wine glass against the wall, was disappointed when it failed to shatter.

She wrote to Annette as if out of the blue, reminding her of the dinner they'd shared. London was looking its best, she said, should they feel like another trip over. Annette took her time then dropped Rose a line to say that they wouldn't be coming this year, then told her of the move to Massachusetts.

We look forward to meeting your sister, she said. *From all we hear, she's a real charmer. Which is no surprise if she's anything like you.*

* * *

Esther expressed little sympathy. 'Get over it,' she said. She could not believe her childhood friend could still be so obsessed.

'She pinched my boyfriend. Now she's after my friends.' This aspect of Rose was not attractive.

'He was never your boyfriend,' said Esther calmly. 'You know that so get a grip.' Put at its bluntest, all Joe'd ever been was a sordid one-night stand.

Rose was a sad pathological case, now behaving increasingly oddly. Rather than getting on with her life and showing the world she no longer cared, it was almost as if she were rapidly regressing. Instead of accepting the true state of things, she still couldn't stand the thought of Lily with Joe.

Alone in her flat, Rose talked to him in an endless pitiful monologue in which she argued her case from every angle. At night, while she tried in vain to sleep, the tape in her head played relentlessly. When she opened her eyes, his presence was there beside her in the room. She loved him, she said, and always would. He had known it from the day they'd first met yet had ruthlessly seduced her then married her sister. She cried, she pleaded, she wanted him back. She was far more suited to him than Lily. She could not allow her sister to steal her friends. Lily was shallow, she pointed out. No possible good could come of such a mismatch. She scolded him for not staying in touch; they were family now so what harm could it do? A couple of times she even wrote but later destroyed the letters.

Hugo remained her devoted slave but now she started to turn on him. She would break their dates on a sudden whim without always bothering to tell him. When he called to check what had happened, she blasted him out.

'Leave me alone,' she snarled when he rang, keeping him dangling for days at a time.

'I don't understand why he sticks around,' said Esther.

'He's an utter drip,' said Rose. 'He gets on my nerves. I can't stand the way he looks at me with those stupid puppy dog eyes.'

'That's not what you said a month ago.'

'Hnnh.' Rose gave an elaborate shrug. She was growing nastier by the second. Esther was starting to wonder why she bothered with her at all.

'You'll miss him when he's gone,' she warned, fearful of where Rose was heading now. Other than Esther, she had no close friends. At work they had started to give her a wide berth.

'He's not going anywhere,' said Rose. The fact was, she didn't care either way. Esther was seriously shocked at how hard she'd become.

Rose wrote boldly to Joe again, sending best wishes to the Gerards and asking for their address. She might have got it from Lily, of course, but that was not part of her current campaign. Jean-Paul and Annette were her friends first, had somehow omitted to let her know where they were living. When Joe didn't answer, she wrote again, enclosing a classified government paper, a ministerial comment on the future of nuclear power in the UK. The least he could do, she calculated, was have the manners to thank her.

After a wait came a note from Lily, catching Rose up on the latest news. The Gerards had arrived and were far more fun than she had ever expected. She and Annette were becoming firm friends and often went shopping together. At the end she had tacked on a scribbled PS. Joe thanked her, it said, for the interesting paper.

'He's totally wasted on her. She's a moron,' shrieked Rose.

Esther, despairing, rolled her eyes, suddenly bored by Rose's behaviour. She had stuck by her since the age of eleven but was now pretty disenchanted. Rose had always been twitchy, even at school, but they'd put it down to her genius. Esther was also bright but solidly grounded. They had been to a film and then Rose had cooked, something she'd simply microwaved, and Esther was starting to say she really must go. Rose interrupted, as she so often did. She seemed to be growing increasingly odd. When it wasn't Joe she was on about, it was some unfortunate in her office who, for whatever minor reason, was getting under her skin.

She listed endless petty grievances, unfailingly trivial in the extreme, things that nobody else would still remember. Something unfortunate someone had said; the way they'd excluded her from some function. Even the fact that the office cleaner had chipped her favourite mug.

'Must go,' said Esther, cutting her short, and went to retrieve her coat.

The bedroom was neat but utterly soulless, as, indeed, was the rest of the flat. Rose was neurotically tidy and obsessive. Esther put on her coat then combed her hair; though far from vain, she'd developed a style that made the best of herself. She could still hear Rose monotonously talking the way she did when she'd had a few drinks. Esther had learnt to block it out; she found it very unsettling. She had had enough of the endless rant which was starting to give her a headache.

She checked her bag then her eye was caught by a silver frame she'd not seen before, positioned beneath the lamp on the bedside table. She picked it up for a closer look and caught her breath in a silent gasp. A wedding group, Joe's and Lily's it seemed, though the bride was missing along with the best man. A closer inspection revealed the cuts, a skilful montage of a beaming couple apparently gazing into each other's eyes.

Joe and Rose, the bridegroom and maid of honour.

26

Annette Gerard was a striking woman with warm brown eyes and a compelling smile. She and Jean-Paul knew each other from high school. They were both thirty-seven, Joe's age. Lily liked her from the moment they met though she wasn't remotely what she'd expected. There was nothing at all imposing about her; she did not thrust her learning in your face. They rented a house in nearby Lowell, only thirty-five minutes away, which meant they could meet quite often for coffee and chats.

Annette liked Lily's exuberance and the fact that she was almost absurdly pretty. She could quite understand why misogynist Joe had succumbed so completely and fallen so hard. Too many of his other colleagues had wives who were brainy but dry as sticks. Lily, or so it seemed, was perpetually laughing. Though she had one complaint: she was lonely and bored. There was nothing in Cambridge that really engaged her and Joe was never around to play. These days all he did was work.

'I can't even have a dog,' she complained, she who had wanted to be a vet. 'He disapproves of domestic pets. What I really want, more than anything else, is a baby.'

But babies can't be relied upon to turn up when they are needed most. Lily, though four years into her marriage, was still only twenty-two.

'Stop beating up on yourself,' said Annette. 'The more you worry, the harder it gets.' She spoke from personal experience though was keeping that to herself. When Lily inquired why the Gerards were childless, she neatly changed the subject.

The four of them met up most weekends since Joe and Jean-Paul were such close friends and had worked together now for eleven years. Jean-Paul was thin, with a neat cropped beard, and favoured blazers and polo necks. He had restless eyes, like a questing thrush. Lily liked him a lot.

Although she was adept at making cakes, she still found it hard to produce several courses on time. The men lounged around in her spacious kitchen that opened into the dining room, watching her struggling with Sunday lunch, assisted by Annette.

Joe pulled the cork out of a bottle of excellent wine.

Lily had problems with the mash; her mother mostly did roast potatoes by dropping them into the pan alongside the bird. She was practising for Thanksgiving Day which, this year, it would be their turn to host. Joe slapped her gently on the rump and told her to get a move on. He hated to see her bungling things; God knows, she had little enough else to do. He passed round the potato chips. He was growing peckish; they all were.

Annette was tactfully slicing beans, occasionally stopping to baste the bird. Joe walked through to the morning room to select some suitable music. What he chose was Bruckner, his current favourite. He had tried to interest Lily but failed. As time went on they had less and less in common.

'Do you still play?' Jean-Paul inquired.

'Very seldom. I don't have the time.'

'A shame,' said Annette. 'You used to be so good.'

'Lily prefers to watch TV. And what my princess wants, she invariably gets.'

His back was still turned so the Gerards weren't sure whether or not he was making mock. Lily, still bashing away at the spuds, said nothing.

At last the meal was ready; she served it up and Jean-Paul gallantly helped hand round the plates.

'Thank you,' she squealed in her little girl voice,

coquettishly flashing her dimples at him although she was growing too old for this schoolgirl behaviour.

If I didn't like Joe so much, thought Annette, I'd be tempted to wring her neck.

It was what the faculty wives all felt. They resented this child with the innocent eyes who found it impossible not to flirt with their husbands.

Jean-Paul, sensing a slight impasse, changed the subject and asked about Rose. How was she liking her job, he inquired. They'd enjoyed the evening they'd spent with her in London.

'Ask him,' said Lily, with a flash of venom, her face all flushed from the oven.

Joe, who was absorbed in the music, conducting with the glass in his hand, appeared impervious to the conversation.

'She keeps on writing him letters,' said Lily. 'Though they haven't been friends since before we met. She always was a pushy cow. I wish she'd leave him alone.'

So much for Miss Sweetness and Light. The Gerards exchanged a significant glance. Jean-Paul had never quite understood what Joe ever saw in Lily.

'Yes, she's pretty,' he had said from the start. 'But far too young for a man like him. No intellectual depth whatsoever. I cannot believe it will last.'

The thing about Rose, for all her faults, was she had that extraordinary brain and a job at the DTI which was sending her rapidly skywards. He could see she was far too intense for most tastes; sympathised entirely with Joe who had told him a little, over the years, about her bizarre obsession. But she'd seemed very nice when they'd finally met her, had gone to such lengths to entertain Joe's friends. And again in London; he had seen a glimpse of her deepseated insecurity. She wasn't the gorgon her sister described but an anxious uncertain woman who just got things wrong.

'In some ways,' he mused as Annette drove him home, 'Rose is more suited to Joe than Lily.' If only she hadn't come on so strong. The poor guy was scared to death.

27

Two years passed and Rose moved up. Was promoted twice and switched to a different department. She was now overseeing economists; in some ways her job and Esther's overlapped. Esther had other things on her mind; encouraged by her illustrious father, she was fighting her first Labour seat. It was Lewisham, south of the river in London, which had always politically been on the cusp. Within a year of the General Election, the sitting member, against the odds, had, with only a minimal warning, defected to the LibDems. Esther and her partner, Meg, uprooted themselves from their Brixton house and moved to Honor Oak Park.

'I hope you'll come and canvass for me. I'm going to need all the help I can get. Even at the best of times, we have only ever been marginal.' The by-election was Esther's chance to sell herself to the electorate as a dress rehearsal for the real event.

Rose said she would and then forgot. These days she was almost totally self-absorbed. If she cared for anyone, it was Esther, though her nose had slightly been put out of joint when Esther shacked up with Meg. Meg was OK, a high school teacher, but Rose felt excluded from their relationship though, if she were honest, it wasn't their fault. She had an open invitation to visit whenever she cared to.

Meanwhile she was still writing to Joe and these days he occasionally answered. They were, after all, now related. And Lily was much too self-involved to care or, possibly, even know. Rose sent him news of their Oxford friends, the few with whom she remained in touch, as well as snippets of information from government sources she thought might interest him. Joe was an eminent nuclear scientist; Rose now had access to privileged files. Should he ever ask, she would give him the world. For now he must make do with crumbs.

These days Jean-Paul seemed perpetually tired; Annette put it down to overwork and kept her eye on him when he wasn't looking. He had also lost weight; his shirts didn't fit and she noticed him constantly hitching up his pants. When she asked if he'd like a new belt for Christmas, he laughed and said he had more than enough. She checked and he'd pulled them in a couple of notches.

She consulted Joe, for so long his best friend. How did he think, she asked, Jean-Paul was looking? Fine, said Joe, who was not observant. He worked long hours, as both of them did, and showed no decrease in his daily performance. They still played tennis together and sometimes golf.

'I think,' he said, 'we could all use a break.' It had been a very long winter. So they planned a skiing weekend in Vermont in a couple of months, before the snow had all gone.

Lily, meanwhile, still moaned to her mum. Joe had become even more remote. He came home late and preoccupied, then shut himself in his study behind closed doors. He seemed no longer to care how she looked, though occasionally blanched when he saw the bills. Thank goodness she had Annette as a friend, though lately even she had become elusive.

'I don't know what's going on,' she complained, 'but Joe spends more and more time with her. She's supposed to be my friend, not his, but lately they seem to be always in corners, talking.' Though Annette was fifteen years older than Lily, she had kept herself in excellent shape with yoga and workouts at the gym as well as a lot of tennis. Her work as a microbiologist left little time for just idling around. Apart from the occasional lunch, they mainly met as a foursome at weekends.

Bunty sighed. She had seen this coming. Her baby girl, whom she cherished so much, was not the intellectual equal of her husband and his friends. She should have married a local boy if Joe hadn't swept her off her feet. She could understand what she'd seen in him. Those dangerous eyes still made her own palms damp. But Joe was decidedly not to be trusted; the signs had been there from the start. She dared not even discuss it with Matthew, he was so protective where the girls were concerned. And since the death of his only son . . . She poured herself a very stiff drink then telephoned Lily to suggest she come home again.

'Why, this time?' Matthew sighed when he heard. He was tired too and needed a break. Although he adored all three of them, there were times they were, frankly, too much.

'She needs to get away from that man.' Bunty was clearly feeling no pain and an urgent smell from the kitchen suggested that something in the oven required attention.

The breaking point came when Lily came home to find Annette's car outside the house and the distant sound of a plangent Schubert sonata. It was nine o'clock. It wasn't like Joe to be entertaining this late on his own, especially when he'd said nothing about it to her. She had been to a cake decorating class, in a last ditch effort to polish her skills in the hope of getting some sort of job in Boston. Her mother was right, she'd too little to do and part-time work would, at least, get her out of the house. She thanked her for offering to pay her fare home but felt that sorting her life out ought to come first.

The lights in the living room were low. She paused in the hall but could hear no conversation. It was ages now since she'd heard Joe play; she sometimes wondered why they kept the piano which took up so much space.

'I'm back,' she called but he kept on playing instead of rushing to greet her, as once he'd have done. So she dumped her bag and checked her hair then opened the door and went inside.

Joe barely raised his eyes to hers but Annette scrambled up and hugged her.

'Shush,' barked Joe so they both sat down and listened until he had finished the piece then, apparently having lost interest, closed the piano.

Annette explained they had met at the lab and he'd brought her back for a spot of supper since Lily was out and so was Jean-Paul, in Boston giving a lecture.

'Shame,' said Lily, with tightened lips. 'We might have travelled together.'

There was something, she felt, they weren't sharing

with her; a sense of conspiracy in the air that had ceased abruptly the second she entered the room. She made her excuses and fled upstairs.

Then called her mother and said she had changed her mind.

28

Lily was losing her looks, Rose thought, not without a twinge of satisfaction. She was twenty-four, no longer a fairy doll. Though also, perversely, it slightly hurt to see her perfect sister in any way flawed. She gave her a routine peck on the cheek which Lily seemed hardly to notice. It wasn't Rose she had come all this way to see. They were up in town on a shopping spree and Bunty had prevailed upon Rose to join them for lunch at Harvey Nichols. It wasn't often the sisters got to meet.

'She is feeling depressed and needs a few hugs. Don't be mean, it's the least you can do. You're hardly ever in touch with her. I don't believe you can't spare her a little of your time.'

Rose gave in. It was easier than having to spell things out to Bunty. Also she couldn't resist the lure of getting an update on Joe. Although these days he occasionally wrote, acknowledging items of news she had sent, she could hardly call it a real correspondence. She didn't even have his email address.

It wasn't Joe, though, Lily had on her mind. To Rose's surprise, it was Annette. There was something going on, Lily thought, from which she felt excluded. Whenever she entered a room where they were, they both shut up.

'Surely not, dear. You're imagining things.' Bunty had never met the Gerards but felt as though she knew them since Annette was now Lily's close friend.

Lily stubbornly shook her head. She suspected some kind of conspiracy. 'Joe's always treated me like a kid. Now she's doing it too.'

But how was Joe? Rose needed to know. She couldn't abide all this casual sniping. There was no way in the world, she was sure, that Annette would betray Jean-Paul.

'The same,' said Lily sulkily, pushing the food about her plate. She was thinner and her skin had lost its translucence.

'What do you mean the same?' asked Rose, biting back her fierce impatience. Lily might look sensational but her conversation still lacked a lot. She still remained the petulant child at heart.

'He seems not to notice me any more. No longer

listens to what I say. Leaves the room in the middle of meals. Sometimes eats in his study.'

All this was balm to Rose's ears but she caught her mother's warning frown and managed not to gloat. She'd had it coming, the little bitch. This was what happened eventually when you punched above your weight.

'He won't even let me have a dog.' The litany went on and on. 'If only I could conceive, he might love me again.'

Ouch. Rose hadn't seen that one coming. She made an excuse and withdrew to the loo. As she smoothed her hair and touched up her eyes, she couldn't help feeling that, just this once, she matched her sister in style, if not in looks. But the bit about conception hurt; she could only handle the agony if she closed her mind to the thought that they might have sex. It all came back in a whoosh of pain, the memories she tried so hard to suppress. The humiliating time they had slept together and the night of the ball when she'd made such a fool of herself. She only prayed he had not told Lily. She could never face any of them again if either story emerged.

'All right?' asked Bunty when Rose returned, restored to her chic and soignée self. 'Have we time for coffee or should we leave?'

Rose had a meeting scheduled for three and was

weary of their empty chatter. Mother and daughter were much the same, their minds set on trivial things. Yet she couldn't quite tear herself away. Perversely, Lily was like a magnet. When she opened her mouth she talked utter rot yet still had the power to hold her sister in thrall.

She thought rapidly then resumed her seat. 'Perhaps just a quick one,' she said. 'You've not told us much about life in the States. How is Joe liking his job?'

'He's not happy,' she crowed to Esther. 'I fear there's trouble in the marriage.'

'Wipe that grin off your face,' said her friend. 'Remember she is your sister.'

They were having a drink at the House of Commons which was where Esther practically lived these days. The pressures of office had slimmed her down; she was half the size she once had been. Also, since Meg, she was dressing much better, had developed a style of her own.

'If he isn't happy he might come home.' Rose hadn't lost her tunnel vision.

'And if he did, your sister would come with him.'

Esther was used to her one-track mind, had given up trying to divert her but had always known there could be no happy ending.

'How's Hugo these days?' She changed the subject

though knew, from her vagueness, that Rose was still focused on Joe.

'Hugo's fine,' Rose said thoughtfully. 'All Joe really needs is the right sort of bait.' The glint in her eye betrayed the fact that she was back into scheming mode. 'Tell me about global warming,' she said. 'What precisely is being done to prevent it?'

Matthew persuaded Rose to come home for a final dinner before Lily left. He wanted his daughters to get on better, was concerned at their falling out. Lily seemed troubled by several things that she wouldn't discuss when her father was there. But he wasn't a fool, had eyes in his head. Something was terribly wrong.

During the meal, Joe called from the States and Lily was gone for quite a while; they could hear her voice on a rising note talking plaintively just out of earshot.

'Poor child,' said Bunty. 'She wants a baby. I told her it often takes longer than this.' It had been three years after Simon's death before she'd conceived again.

'She wants it all on a plate,' snapped Rose. 'What did she ever do to deserve it?' Primped and flirted and acted the child; she hadn't a brain in her head.

Bunty caught Matthew's eye; they concurred. She knew his concern was as great as her own. They should never have let their precious child marry that much older man.

Rose swept off to clear the plates, returning as Lily slammed down the phone. 'He doesn't understand me,' she sobbed through uncontrollable tears.

'Let him go. He's mine,' hissed Rose, too low for her parents to overhear.

'You must be out of your mind,' Lily snapped. 'What possible interest could he have in you?'

'Now then, girls,' said Matthew, appearing. 'What say we all have an early night? We have to be up at the crack for Lily's plane.'

'You're right,' he said to Bunty later. 'Something's amiss which we have to control.'

'If only Rose had a man of her own,' Bunty sighed.

Nuclear physics. Of course that was it. As Esther outlined the latest thinking, Rose's mind was hatching a devious plan. Climate change was likely to be the greatest of many significant challenges for all humanity in the future unless something drastic was done. Nuclear power, among other things, despite the strong opposition of Greenpeace, might well be required to prevent the planet's destruction. It generated, Esther explained, very low carbon emissions though the Greens were largely opposed to it because of the problems with radioactive waste.

'What's required,' said Esther weightily, as PPS to the Secretary of State, 'are nuclear plants with a different design, with safety features not currently used and, most of all, fuel that cannot be made into bombs.'

Esther had always been deeply committed, genuinely cared about saving the world. Had won her seat exclusively on that platform.

'Why are you smiling?' she suddenly asked, observing the gleam in Rose's eye. 'And why this interest in global warming? What do you know about the subject?'

'Not a great deal,' said Rose, still smiling. 'But I know a man who does.'

29

Rose pestered Esther until she cracked. When she wanted something, she didn't let up, as Esther, from long experience, knew to her cost. The job was major and international. Whoever they chose would be London-based and part of a high-level government team reporting direct to the top.

'Now not a word,' she hissed at Rose, 'or else you'll land me in deepest shit.' Her ministerial post was confidential.

Rose just smiled but her mind was racing, already formulating a plan that could, if it worked, solve a number of crucial problems. Joe was seeing too much of Annette; Lily was missing her mother. If she came back home, she could get a job which might put an end to her endless whining and bring her into contact with men her own age. Joe, repatriated, might relax and recognise there were other options. Could re-establish

163

his Oxford links and play the piano again.

'What's up with Rose? She seems very bouncy?' Matthew noticed a very marked change.

'I think it's just that Lily has gone,' said his wife.

'We can't keep meeting like this,' said Joe. 'What if Jean-Paul should become suspicious?'

'He thinks I am at a yoga class,' said Annette, who was looking very strained. The past few weeks had taken their toll. Too little sleep and a guilty conscience were starting to show in her face.

Joe leaned across and touched her arm. 'Courage,' was all he said. He caught the bartender's eye and beckoned him over.

'I can't stay long.' She was late as it was and hated deceiving her trusting husband. They had married early and never had secrets before.

'What are we going to do?' she asked, gazing imploringly at Joe. He'd been her rock and mainstay these past few months.

He gripped her hand. 'We will see it through and not give up till we've found a solution. You know how much you mean to me. I will never let you down.'

'You are still the only person I trust.'

'Soon, I'm afraid, he will have to be told.'

'Not until we are totally sure. Does Lily know?' she asked.

'No,' said Joe. She was indiscreet. And this concerned just the three of them.

'I couldn't cope without you,' said Annette, rubbing the tears from her eyes.

'You'll never have to. I swear,' said Joe, firmly entwining his fingers in hers. 'I'm in for the long run. You know you can count on me.'

Lily was seething when Joe walked in and almost hurled the supper at him. 'Why didn't you bloody ring?' she shrieked. 'You have ruined my casserole.'

'Grow up,' he said. 'And don't scream like that. We don't want the neighbours coming round.' If she'd only develop a life of her own, he would find her less irksome to live with. He hadn't the stomach to argue with her, nor did he feel the remotest guilt. If the food was ruined, it wasn't his fault. He would take up a snack to his study.

'You never talk to me any more.' She watched him as he flicked through the mail.

His withering glance was enough to freeze mercury. 'You rarely say anything worth hearing.'

'Where have you been? You never say.'

'Working,' he said and closed the study door.

Jean-Paul looked tired when Annette got home, with prominent circles beneath his eyes. She offered him food but he said he wasn't hungry.

'I think I'll have an early night.' His face was gaunt and his beard turning grey. He had aged ten years in the past few weeks. She suppressed the desire to cry.

She crouched beside him as he lay in his chair and settled her head on his chest. Please don't leave me, she begged without saying a word.

'How was yoga?'

'Good,' she said. 'She is teaching us a new exercise.' The secret she carried was burning her up but still she couldn't divulge it.

'Lily called.'

'What did she want?' There had been a time when they spoke every day.

'She didn't say. But sounded quite lonely, I thought.'

Joe's child bride was all very well, good company when she felt in the mood but impossibly selfish when things didn't go her way.

'I'll call her tomorrow.' Annette was tired too. This subterfuge was destroying her. The only thing she cared about now was keeping the truth from Jean-Paul. It was one reason she stayed away from Lily who hadn't the sense she was born with.

When Lily timidly tapped on the door, she found Joe hunched in his reading chair though the book on his lap was open but turned face down. There was music playing, a sorrowful dirge that she thought she knew but couldn't quite place. Unlike her erudite older sister's, her knowledge of music was scant.

'Are you coming to bed? It's almost twelve.' Even when Joe was alone here, reading, she felt like an intruder.

'Soon,' he said and stretched out his arm to catch her wrist and draw her closer. 'I should never have married you,' he said. 'It was selfish of me. I'm sorry.'

'Why?' she asked, sliding on to his knee, a reflex from when she was Daddy's girl. That was the problem with Lily's life: she had never entirely grown up. First her father had doted on her and then this man who was so much older. If her brother had lived, she'd have had a more fitting role model.

'I feel I have let you down,' said Joe. 'By not providing the things you want. You can have a dog if you really insist but it won't solve your problem long term.'

She snuggled her head beneath his chin, the way she had always done with her dad, and waited for Joe to finish his silent brooding. In this sort of mood it was always bad news. The man had a talent for bringing her down.

'Please let's go to bed,' she said. 'And finish this in the morning.'

*　　*　　*

They were still in bed when the doorbell rang, both pretending to be asleep. Lily had a strong premonition that she wasn't going to like what Joe had to say. She looked at the clock; it was not yet seven.

'I'll go,' she said and was out of bed before he was fully awake.

The courier wore his visor down but pushed it up when she opened the door.

'I am sorry to call so early,' he said. 'But they told me it was important.'

He needed Joe's signature, hers wouldn't do, and he refused to tell her why this should be. 'Confidential,' was all she could get out of him.

'Wait down here.' She invited him in and left him standing alone in the hall still holding the thin buff envelope that was so urgent.

'What is it?' Joe hated to be disturbed and came down grumbling and fastening his robe.

'Government business,' said the man and gave him a clipboard to sign.

Joe signed and received the envelope, scratching his head in disbelief at the portcullis crest and address: *10 Downing Street.*

30

He was coming home. She had pulled it off. Rose was out of her mind with joy. She daren't tell Esther who'd find out soon enough. What she had done was not pulling strings; she had simply dropped Joe's name and credentials into an appropriate ear and then withdrawn and quietly watched it happen. She had not revealed the family tie; the chances were the link would forget it was she who had put forward his name in the first place. Then followed what seemed an interminable wait while she held her breath hoping he'd swallow the bait. The first she knew was when Bunty called to tell her that Lily was coming home.

'Joe has got this amazing new job. Which at present is still under wraps.'

Rose smiled with relief and released her breath. She felt quite dizzy with satisfaction. She had not believed he could be so easily snared. From what Lily said when she'd last been home, he was seeing too much of Annette these days. Space between them could only be good and Rose would in future be able to keep a close eye on him herself. Not to mention the fact she would see him again; the thought made her positively giddy.

Lily came first, to find them a home, and, with Bunty's help, trawled the upmarket areas close to where he'd be working, in Smith Square.

'Dad says he'll probably get a knighthood.' Lily's spirits seemed well restored. She had put on some weight, which suited her, and her skin once more was flawless. She was wearing pale blue and her hair was lighter; it floated round her face in ethereal curls. 'Can't you just see it?' She struck a pose. 'Lady Markovich.'

Rose faked delight to disguise her scowl, itching to slap the smile off her sister's face. Still, if having Joe back meant Lily too, it was worth the sacrifice. She could hardly wait to see him again. It had been six years, since the wedding.

They rented a flat in Pimlico in a handsome Victorian building. Their furniture was shipped over and quickly installed. Still no Joe who was winding things up. He was far too pressured to move till all was sorted.

'What if he doesn't like it?' asked Rose, who couldn't

resist dropping in all the time. The great thing was, they were now within walking distance.

'He'll just have to lump it. It's done now,' said Lily, back to her old exuberant form, relieved to be in London, close to her mother.

'What will you do about a job?' It was vital she shouldn't just hang around, fretting about the baby she longed for but seemed unable to have. Rose had only Joe's interests at heart. She was also anxious that Lily should not conceive.

'I'm thinking of opening a hat shop,' said Lily.

'Hats!' said Rose, who'd not worn one in years. Not since she'd left school, in fact, not even to Lily's wedding.

'They are back in fashion,' Lily assured her. She steeped herself in the glossy magazines. 'Next season's hottest accessory, in fact.' She had talked it over with Joe and her parents and Bunty was keen to become involved. Lily had found the ideal location, in a King's Road side street, a block away from where Bunty had run her boutique. Matthew offered to help with the costs but Lily, with smug satisfaction, said no. Her husband insisted on being the sole provider.

'I'll give him that, he is good to me, allows me to have whatever I want.' She'd already taken him at his word by blowing a fortune in Sloane Street.

Rose continued to hold her tongue and not let Lily

get under her skin. If this was the price she had to pay in order to be near Joe again, it was worth it.

'I knew you were up to something,' Esther scolded. 'It has to be you behind this appointment. You know nothing good can come of it. It is bound to end in tears.'

'He's the right man for the job,' said Rose, coolly dismissing all accusations. 'I don't deny it had crossed my mind but these decisions, as you very well know, are made at the highest level.'

Esther snorted. At times like this she couldn't believe she'd remained so loyal. All Rose ever cared about was herself. As Meg pointed out, she was an inveterate user. But she seemed pretty competent at her job; her department was held in the highest esteem. She functioned well in the civil service which was the mainstay of Parliament.

'Have you seen him yet?'

Rose shook her head. 'He doesn't arrive till Friday.'

They were all invited for Sunday lunch though Lily was doubtful he'd feel inclined to drag himself out to Twickenham quite so soon. Instead she booked a table for five in a classy restaurant in Pimlico.

'You'll understand, I'm sure,' she said, 'if we keep it short and sweet.'

Rose, in a fever of anticipation, ransacked her

wardrobe for something to wear. She had learnt a lot, in the past six years, about style and presentation.

'There is no point trying to upstage Lily.' Esther was still very much on her case. 'Apart from the fact she is nine years younger, she's also his legal wife.'

Rose ignored her, as she always had, and continued her hunt for the perfect look. Since Lily was partial to girlish pastels, she settled on understated black. With her grandmother's pearls which he'd seen before but would not, she hoped, remember.

He'd aged but still looked extremely good when they all shuffled into the restaurant as the guests of Lily and Joe. In order to heighten the impact of reunion Rose deliberately let her parents go first. He was tall and lean, with the same thick hair, slicked back and distinguished because of the grey. His eyes were pouchy but still intense. They narrowed with something that could be surprise when he caught his first glimpse of her.

'Rose,' he said, extending both hands to envelop her fingers between his own. She raised herself on her toes and kissed his cheek.

He looked what he was, a man of distinction returned from exile to save his country, the weary cynicism in his eyes belied by the sensuous curve of his mouth. His cheeks were hollow and heavily lined. He could have been ten years more than his actual age. Lily, with her now platinum hair, hovered beside him, smiling brightly, wearing something gauzy in mauve with serious silver earrings. Rose, by contrast, looked cutting-edge chic. Her hair was glossy and impeccably bobbed; she had kept her figure, was still a trim size eight.

The magnetism had in no way diminished. When he looked at her, she could not avert her eyes. She felt as though they were there alone, like the very first time she'd caught sight of him in that smoky Oxford bar, fifteen years ago.

'Rose,' he said in a softer tone and she knew from the way he held her gaze that he'd not forgotten a thing.

31

It was the faces that sometimes got Rose down; they stared at her from inanimate things, especially when she came home late from the office. Most of them were innocuous, the tiger face in the battered cushion, the quizzical smile on the shampoo bottle or the marching troops in the wooden surround of the bath. When she was tired, though, or feeling upset, a creeping menace could infiltrate. The lampshade hanging above her bed took on the shape of a vampire bat; the dressing gown casually tossed on a chair assumed the crouching outline of a panther. She'd had these illusions all her life but lately they'd grown more threatening. She had never discussed them with anyone else. The colour of music was weird enough and the numbers floating in the air.

The fact that Joe now lived so close affected her more than she had foreseen. There were nights when she couldn't settle so roamed the streets. Inevitably she'd end up outside his block, on the chance she might meet him on his way home. Just a glimpse would be enough; her expectations weren't high. She would even occasionally ring the bell with some cooked-up story about passing by. Invariably Lily answered because he was out.

Now that Lily was back in town and sharpening up her business plans, the sisters were getting on better. The difference in age that had once seemed so great had narrowed now they were both adult and Lily had the advantage by being married. Though Rose by no means cherished the companionship, she knew her parents would approve and, with luck, it might also help bring her closer to Joe. Lily, who never could make decisions, relied on Rose's superior knowledge the way she had done, in childhood, on her father's. Matthew and Rose were much alike while Lily was a replica of her mother.

This new close harmony worked for Rose, enabling her to keep tabs on Joe without intruding too much into the marriage. Often, in those late-night sessions, he'd arrive home wearily from work and join them for a glass or so before putting Rose in a cab. She was crazy, he said, to be out alone, especially this late at night.

'This is my city,' was her reply. 'I feel totally safe.'

Joe had mellowed, was less abrupt and more inclined to listen to her. The antipathy he had once displayed seemed to have faded after he married Lily. He respected Rose's intelligence as well as her take on current affairs. Intellectually, they were perfectly matched and had a great deal in common.

'What are you two talking about?' Lily often appeared put out when she caught them privately laughing.

'Nothing special. Just politics. Your sister has an excellent insight into how this country is run.'

At least Rose was preferable to Annette who seemed no longer part of their lives. This move to London had served them all and was helping ease the tension between the sisters.

'How are the Gerards getting on?' asked Rose while Lily prepared their supper. They were gossiping in Joe's study, out of earshot.

'Things aren't too good,' he said, suddenly grave. 'I'd rather not mention it to Lily but Jean-Paul is seriously ill. He has leukaemia.'

Rose was shocked. She had liked him a lot, not only because he was Joe's best friend. The Gerards had been very kind to her and made her feel she belonged.

'Does he know?'

'Not yet. Annette has kept it from him in the hope

that the tests might turn out benign. Of course he knows there is something wrong but she feels the truth might sap his strength and remove his incentive to fight. It has been a struggle because they're so close but Annette believes it's the way he'd want it to be. I have to trust her.'

'How long does he have?'

'Not long,' said Joe. 'I'd be obliged if you'd not tell Lily. I don't want her making a fuss and upsetting them both.'

Hence the secrecy. Rose was relieved, could sacrifice Jean-Paul for peace of mind. She was also chuffed that Lily didn't know.

The plans for a hat shop were going smoothly with considerable help from both parents. Bunty spent most of the week in town, occasionally staying overnight, leaving Matthew to fend for himself in the luxury of a house devoid of chatter. He had negotiated the lease and was also handling the paperwork. Chelsea rents were premium but Matthew reckoned the gamble worth it. Especially since it provided work for two pairs of idle hands.

They threw themselves into their market research, with expeditions all over town to view what the competition was doing before they invested in stock. Bunty, having run a boutique, knew the basics of how it was done and phoned round acquaintances to call in a few old favours. They planned to buy in but also to make; both were proficient with a needle and the part that excited Lily most was the idea of designing their own creations. Both acquired a new lease of life; Lily had fretted for far too long. And it helped take her mind off the pregnancy issue.

The shop was small and neat and bright, on a busy corner of a friendly lane which had the feeling of a cosy village high street. Lily fixed the window herself, using the decorative skills she'd acquired while doing all that icing. She hired a girl as a runaround, to collect the fabrics and drop off the hats, and stood behind the counter herself when she wasn't backstage, sewing. All the designing was done at home; she converted a bedroom into a workshop. Soon the place was awash with colour, with rows of faceless wig-stands like decapitated heads.

'Do you ever play in public?' asked Rose. Joe's piano was still in storage since there wasn't room in the London flat and he didn't want it damaged.

'Never,' he said. That was all behind him, part of his long-forgotten youth. He had taken to wearing reading glasses which gave him an added distinction.

'Do you still hear music in colour?' he asked, recalling how much he had rattled her. There were things about Rose that he found intriguing; he still hadn't figured her out.

'I rarely have time to listen to music,' she said.

She took them to Pizza on the Park, to sample the evening cabaret. 'You could be doing this,' she said. 'It's a shame you stopped. You were good.'

'You're talking about my misspent youth. I left all that behind when I settled down.'

'So instead you're changing the world?' she quipped.

'Something like that,' he said.

At forty he was a striking man, with brooding eyes and a dour expression that lightened into a heartfelt chuckle when something made him smile. His moods were unpredictable; not even Lily could sense their swing. Much of the time he seemed withdrawn, lost in a cerebral world of his own, bored by the mundane trivia of daily life. He resembled, Rose realised, her father a bit, with a need to shut himself off from the world. Was that where the strong attraction lay? Perhaps.

She ached to kiss that chiselled mouth and still had carnal dreams about that barely remembered night they had shared. She was sometimes aware of him watching her, eyes narrowed behind a plume of smoke. He smoked as much as he ever had, made no attempts to quit. It was part of the essence of who he was, a man whose brain was superior. And one who didn't give a damn.

Rose returned to her silent flat, aware of the faces watching her, feeling their eyes pursuing her round the room. At last she could lower the cool façade and let the force of her anguish rip. She loved him as much as she ever had and it was torture.

32

As Rose progressed up the chain of command, inevitably she encountered Ann Cole again. Ann was approaching retirement age but her abrasiveness had in no way diminished, and when Rose moved back as department head she found her as forthright as ever.

'I believe in speaking my mind,' she bragged. 'In calling a spade a shovel.'

She was short and sturdy with the same cropped white hair and a critical stare that put people off. Her office was close to the main double doors which gave her an unimpeded view of the department's comings and goings. If Rose wasn't there by the crack of nine, usually due to a breakfast meeting, Ann's brash voice would trumpet out: 'You're late. Did you oversleep?' Then she suffered the ignominy of Ann's triumphant cackle.

Rose found this attitude disrespectful, though there wasn't much she could do about it without a head-on confrontation.

'Get on with your work,' she'd snap. 'And if you've finished, I'll find you more.'

'She's only jealous,' a colleague explained. 'She was cock of the walk before you came. She isn't half as bright as you and she knows it.'

Still, Rose found Ann's hostility unnerving, though made a point of never letting it show.

When word got round that Joe Markovich, the distinguished MIT physicist, was married to Rose's sister, Ann was in clover. She was keen to know how he'd got the job since she'd not seen his name on any list and it did seem an odd coincidence that he'd turned up unannounced.

'I have no idea,' Rose told her crisply. 'The Department of the Environment brought him in.' Where her best friend was, it was widely known, PPS to the Secretary of State. Ann remained mute but her beady eyes didn't miss a thing.

'What's he like? As smart as they say?' Once into her stride, there was no deflecting Ann. She was like a terrier on the job, would not desist until she had cornered her prey.

'He is certainly very clever,' said Rose. 'Los Alamos before MIT. I suspect the main thing going for him is that he's British by birth.' Northern, too, though she didn't add that. Joe had always been reticent about his Geordie roots.

'Hmm,' said Ann, still not satisfied. And made a point of discussing him whenever she knew Rose could hear.

Rose liked it that Joe was making his mark, though still felt possessive about him. She occasionally had to caution Ann about too much uncensored chat. Quite apart from the family connection, Joe was here on a sensitive mission, reporting only to his chief of staff, the PM.

She closed her ears to Ann's mutterings; would not tolerate gossip in her department.

The news from America wasn't good. Jean-Paul was declining fast. He now knew what was wrong with him so Joe felt obliged to let Lily know as well.

'Why didn't you tell me before?' she cried. 'I could have gone over to be with Annette.' Despite any insecure feelings she had, she hated it most that she had been excluded.

'She didn't want too many people knowing for fear of him finding out,' said Joe. 'It was a tough decision but one she felt was for the best.'

'You knew,' said Lily accusingly.

'Jean-Paul and I have always been close.' Which, to Lily, meant he cared more about him than her.

'Let's not turn this into a fight.' He sighed as he so often did these days. 'I have told Annette I'll be over as soon as I can.'

Lily insisted on going too and there wasn't a lot he could say to dissuade her. She wanted to be there for Annette; the hats, she said, could wait. It was true the women had been good friends before Lily started acting up. Bunty offered to see to the shop which would be like old times. She was keen on the idea of running a business again.

'Rose can help me in her spare time.' After all, she had little social life. Since Joe arrived she had abandoned Hugo.

Rose wasn't keen, knowing nothing of hats. But, since this was a family affair, she grudgingly agreed.

'You don't have to work in the shop,' said Bunty. 'Just lend a hand on the business side.' With a brain like hers, it should not take much time and might increase her awareness. It was long overdue that she learnt to put others' needs before her own.

It would also mean she had access to Lily's flat. That was where the ledgers and orders were kept, since Lily worked on them after closing hours, overseen occasionally by her father.

'How long will you be gone?' asked Rose, suddenly animated.

'As long as it takes,' said Joe, clearly very upset.

Faced with the prospect of losing his friend, he was ashen-faced, his eyes like pits. Rose ached inside to see his obvious grieving.

'Stay as long as you need to,' said Bunty. 'The pair of us together can cope.' She saw herself back in the Swinging Sixties, once more a glamorous icon of the King's Road.

Rose fancied herself in paradise, sanctioned keeper of Joe's keys, able to come and go whenever she wanted. Each night she went direct to the shop where Bunty would still be closing up, collected the relevant paperwork and took it back to his flat. Now and again her mother came too but mostly she went straight home to Matthew. He wasn't accustomed to having to cope; she felt the least she should do was eat with him.

Rose was free to explore at her leisure, snooping in cupboards and opening drawers, ferreting out as much about Joe and his life as she possibly could. Since the flat was spacious (he was very well paid) they each kept a separate dressing room in addition to his study and Lily's workroom. Room enough, as she'd noted before, to put plenty of space between them.

Lily had always collected stuff; her boudoir resembled an Eastern bazaar. Most of it was cheap and naff; Rose would have binned the lot. The workroom next door was not much better, an overflow of the same. There were rolls of felt in assorted colours, muslin and feathers for the trims. Velvet ribbon and ornate net lay around all over the place awaiting Lily's mercurial inspiration. The faceless heads on their wooden blocks stood in colourful serried rows, reminding Rose of a Wimbledon crowd, eager for the start of play. She tried on several half-finished creations, pulling suitable faces in the glass. There was no disputing the fact that her sister could sew. The craft and energy once used on cakes she now employed in a more lasting way. If hats were her thing, thought Rose, she would certainly buy one. One especially caught her fancy, a 1940s slouch-brimmed fedora, as worn by Garbo and Bergman in their heyday. She anchored it carefully on to her head. Nice, she thought. Ideal for a seduction.

By contrast, Joe's dressing room was austere. His well-pressed suits hung in orderly rows, his shoes lined up beneath them. Gone was all trace of the rakish youth; the man who now moved in government circles possessed both style and taste. Rose ran her fingers over his clothes, feeling the quality of the cloth, appreciating the cut. She took out his jackets and tried them on, pressing her cheek against each one, closing her eyes to inhale his integral essence. She opened his drawers and went through his shirts, immaculately starched and ironed, though not by Lily. *Oh, Joe*. It was almost too much to bear. This was the life that should have been hers, snatched away by a magpie child who took whatever she wanted.

She had also been through Lily's things and found her diaphragm left behind. Which must mean that she still hoped to conceive, perhaps without Joe's knowledge. The thought made her crazy. She longed to destroy, to take her sister by her plump little throat and squeeze until the eyes popped out of her skull. All her life she had been indulged; now she had very much overstepped the mark.

She might have had almost any man with her film star looks and radiant smile. Instead she had chosen the only one Rose would ever want.

After she'd brought the books up to date, she would eat a snack at the kitchen table, pour a slug of Joe's favourite bourbon and take it into his study to watch the news. The place had started to feel like home; she would miss it when they returned. It was warm and quietly luxurious, with polished floors and thick pile rugs and close-fitting double glazing that cut out all sound. Outside the streets were slashed with rain and Rose was tired from a heavy day. She wasn't likely to find a cab and hadn't brought an umbrella. She knew if Joe and Lily were here they'd stop her walking home on her own. They would make her stay over; she was, after all, doing them a big favour.

So she slept that night in the master bed, luxurious to the nth degree, beneath an elegant canopy with sheets of purest silk. The bath was marble, to match the drapes. There was even a speaker in the shower. She selected a pair of Joe's pyjamas which, though too large, brought her closer to him. Then she snuggled down in the swansdown pillows and dreamt she was safe in his arms.

At ten past seven she woke abruptly to the unwelcome click of a key in a lock. Someone had let themselves in; she couldn't think who.

It wasn't them; they'd have let her know. She rushed to the window and peered round the blind but the unseen intruder was already inside. The maid, perhaps, though surely not this early. Rose rapidly scrambled into her clothes, praying she wouldn't be caught in their bed. In the morning light even she could see she had grossly invaded their privacy. There wasn't time to unearth her comb, so she used her fingers to smooth her hair then boldly opened the door and ventured out.

A figure was outlined against the light, quietly sorting through the mail. She looked up, surprised, when Rose made her presence known.

'I'm Mrs Markovich's sister,' said Rose. 'I stayed the night having missed my train. Who are you and what are you doing here?'

The girl was slight and dark and pretty, wearing a raincoat and sensible shoes. 'Sorry if I disturbed you,' she said. 'I'm Sukey, here to collect Dr Markovich's mail.'

33

She mentioned the girl when Lily rang, casually making light of it. She had bumped into someone called Sukey. Young and good-looking.

'Oh,' said Lily. 'That bloody PA.' An ugly note crept into her voice. Sukey was always hanging around these days. Back home, in the States, before he got posh, Joe had never needed these ego props. 'I was all the help he required,' she sniffed, clearly quite put out. She had rung to say they'd be home on Sunday. Sadly, Jean-Paul had passed away. She would have liked to stay on longer but Joe had important meetings.

Rose tried dropping the name to Ann, knowing she would get chapter and verse. Sukey Khan, the department's Suzie Wong.

'At one time she worked for us,' she said. 'Made herself irreplaceable. So was shunted upstairs to ministerial level. Why?' she asked. 'Is there anything wrong?

I believe these days she works for your brother-in-law.'

No flies on Ann. Rose shook her head. 'I just heard her vaguely mentioned,' she said. 'And wondered.'

Ann, however, was worse than a leech. 'They say she has quite a reputation. If I were you I'd warn your sister to keep close tabs on her.'

So Rose asked Esther who heaved a sigh. 'You just can't leave it alone,' she said. 'How can it possibly matter to you who Joe has on his team?'

It was as she'd feared. Rose was still obsessed. The more she heard, the worse it became. Esther really worried for her. Who knew where it might all lead?

Meanwhile, Bunty was worrying too. Lily was home but still wouldn't let up. It was terribly sad about Jean-Paul and she and Annette had patched things up but she still had the nagging feeling that Joe didn't love her. He was working harder than ever before, kept longer hours and was impossible to pin down. When Bunty delicately probed about babies, Lily burst into tears.

'I should never have married him,' she said. 'Now I don't believe he ever loved me.'

Which was rather what Bunty had always thought but never liked to mention before. After seven years she saw how mismatched they were. She did what she could to cheer Lily up. At least the shop was taking off. Their timing had been entirely spot on. Hats were the new hottest thing.

With Lily back, Rose was off the hook though she still had a habit of dropping in. She envied the closeness shared by her mother and sister.

Curiosity prompted her to find out more about Sukey Khan. It seemed she was quite well known throughout the department. Joe was certainly satisfied. When she dropped the name, his eyes lit up. She was, he said, an excellent worker on whom he had learnt to rely.

'What exactly is her role in your life?'

'She runs it for me,' he said.

Ann reported they'd been seen together on several occasions, having lunch. 'They looked closer than boss and PA,' she remarked with a smirk.

Rose snapped at her to mind her own business. Idle gossip did nothing but harm. But she wandered into Joe's office one day, at a time when she knew he was out of town, to take a closer look at this possible rival. Sukey was seated at the computer, seemingly absorbed in her work. She smiled with unfeigned pleasure when Rose walked in.

'Where's Joe?'

'In Harrogate, making a speech. He won't be back till late afternoon. Is there anything I can do for you?' she asked.

'No,' said Rose. 'It's family business. I'd forgotten he wasn't here. How are you getting on?' she asked. 'I hope he's treating you well.'

Sukey was slight and androgynous-looking, as un-developed as a little boy. Her skin was lucid, like alabaster. Her smile was enigmatic. There was something not quite English about her that added to her exotic allure. 'I love it here,' she said. 'He's a marvellous boss.'

You'll get nowhere, thought Rose, by sucking up. The girl clearly remembered that they'd met before. She offered Rose a coffee which she declined.

'Is there a message?'

'No,' said Rose. 'It's family business, as I said.'

She never told Lily she had sought out Sukey but, from that instant, was hot on her case. Any woman getting too close to Joe spelt potential disaster.

Esther thought she was out of her mind. He wouldn't be that stupid, she said. The eyes of the world were on him now; one unconsidered step could wreck his career.

Hmm, said Rose, still unconvinced. She wasn't risking any woman setting her cap at Joe.

'What has happened to poor old Hugo? You don't seem to mention him any more.' Bunty had always liked him a lot, secretly nurturing hopes for the future. It seemed all wrong to have one daughter married and the other, nine years older, still on the shelf. Rose seemed even more tense these days. Bunty hoped it had nothing to do with Joe.

'Oh, he's still around.' It was no big deal. They occasionally met at the Festival Hall. They no longer, however, made music together, as both were so much absorbed in their separate careers.

'Bring him to us for Sunday lunch.' Bunty was not one to give up trying. Hugo had lovely manners and had always seemed sweet on Rose.

Rose simply shrugged. She couldn't care less. Her mind, these days, was preoccupied.

They were seated together round the kitchen table, Lily and Bunty making hats while Rose, sipping wine, was merely looking on. She had dropped in on her way home from work, pretending she needed to talk to her mother but really on the off chance of seeing Joe. She kept glancing covertly at the clock and Bunty, nobody's fool, knew why though Lily, as usual, was steeped in her own complaints. There was still no sign of the longed-for baby. She was wondering now about IVF.

'I'll do whatever it takes,' she wailed. 'Can't bear to think my youth is slipping away.'

Rose snorted. Lily was twenty-six with the brain and behaviour of a tiresome child. She wanted to tell her to get a life but was sick of repeating herself.

'Oh, come now, dear, it's too soon for that.' Bunty, with the most minuscule stitches, was applying net to a saucy cocktail hat. She held it up to show it off then plonked it on Rose's head to judge the effect. 'That really suits you. Shall I make one for you?'

'Where on earth would she wear it?' asked Lily with the smallest soupçon of spite.

Inflamed by her sister's bitchiness and desperately hoping for Joe's return, Rose helped herself to more wine then wandered about. In the cluttered workroom, with its half-finished hats, she tried on the handsome fedora again, anchoring it with an eight-inch ornate hatpin. It definitely gave her a Garbo look, her most striking feature, her cat-like eyes, accentuated now by the sloping brim. She pouted her lips and struck a pose; it made her feel like a femme fatale. She strained for the sound of Joe's key in the lock. He was two hours overdue.

She'd have liked to show the effect to her mother but would not allow Lily the chance to snipe so removed the pin and regretfully placed the hat back on its block. She must leave soon, had no further excuse for lingering, simply in the way. She had not been invited to stay for a meal which was the height of rudeness. She wondered what could be keeping Joe, shuddered to think it might be Sukey. The idea of them together made her crazy.

She clenched her fists, forgetting the hatpin, and drove the point into the palm of her hand. Dear God, it hurt, was positively lethal.

'Do you have any plasters?' she shouted.

'In my bathroom,' said Lily, her mouth full of pins.

'Do you need any help?' called her mother.

'No thanks,' said Rose through gritted teeth, her thumb pressed down hard to prevent the bleeding, hating them both for caring so little about her.

Lily's bathroom was its usual mess, makeup and tissues all over the place and a towel, still wet from the shower, dumped on the floor. She located a plaster and patched up her hand, then touched up her eyes in case Joe should appear and used Lily's brush to smooth her hair into place.

There were moments she really hated her sister though, right now, she hated Sukey more. She had dropped the hatpin into her pocket but now transferred it to her sleeve, buttoning the cuff on a tighter hole to prevent it from doing more damage. A plan was forming; her eyes grew hard. She looked around among Lily's clutter, selected one of her many lipsticks and dropped it into her pocket.

'I think I'll be off,' she said. He wasn't coming.

34

The walk was short, a mere fifteen minutes, and the evening unseasonably mild and clear. Yet, in that time, Rose worked herself into a lather of resentment. The idea of Joe with anyone else was almost more than she could bear. Marrying Lily was bad enough but at least she knew it wasn't working out. Sukey Khan was a brand new threat. The memory of that pert little face was turning her psychotic.

She thought of Ann with her knowing looks and certainty she was always right. She would love to find out that Joe was up to no good. Rose switched on the lamps and Radio 3 to dispel the cavernous silence. There was something hollow about the flat, as if it had never been properly lived in. No one had phoned but they rarely did; even Hugo seemed to have given up. Lately she had begun to suspect he was seeing someone else.

She poured more wine then raked through the fridge in a futile search for something to eat. It was selfish of Lily, mean-spirited too, not to have insisted that she stay. Bunty was there and soon also Joe, assuming he would come home some time. All Rose had was some staleish bread. She slotted two slices into the toaster and opened a can of beans.

Throughout that night she twisted and turned, unable to settle or get to sleep, tortured by the image of Joe with that girl. Ann's gossip was often wide of the mark but its general thrust usually had some basis. She would pick up an innuendo and worry it to death. Beyond the office her life was blank; she had lived with her widowed mother until she died. She was generally known for her acid tongue though some believed it concealed a generous heart. Rose only knew her as a troublemaker who definitely had it in for Joe, although she suspected the actual target was herself. She didn't know why; their paths rarely crossed. The work they did ran mainly on parallel lines. Rose could only think Ann's attitude derived from the spectre of thwarted ambition.

If Ann were right, should Lily be told? That was the question obsessing Rose now. If Joe was unfaithful, Lily should get a divorce. It wasn't too late: she still had her looks and a second marriage might give her the children she longed for. The adrenalin released by this realisation made Rose sit up and switch on the light. It was clear to her now; divorce was the obvious answer. Her heart was pounding, her palms were damp. Till now she had never looked forward that far. She only knew that Joe should be hers, had done so right from the start. Lily had just been a passing whim, due to her startling looks.

She couldn't sleep; no question of that even though it was only a quarter to five. She threw back the covers and paced the room, her heart beating so fast she feared it might explode. Joe was her fate; had always been. No one would come between them again. She had finished the wine so fixed a martini. She needed to make a plan.

Lily was the least of Rose's concerns. The principal target now was the treacherous Sukey. Ann might help get rid of her with her vicious gossip and spiteful tongue since carrying on in government circles was severely frowned upon. But catching them at it would not be enough; then Joe might well go off with the girl. She was even younger than Lily was now, the way he obviously liked them. Rose drained the glass and replenished it. The more she drank, the crazier she became.

She thought about how Joe had treated her, the

snubs, the slights and ill-concealed sneers, the way he had publicly sent her up and privately abused her. She had offered herself to him on a plate – the memory still made her cringe with shame – and he had responded by marrying her sister. She was breathless now with pent-up rage, in a mood to do him serious harm. Yet she still loved him to distraction, could not imagine a future without him in it.

If she couldn't have him, then nobody would. It was time to stake her claim.

He did come home. Rose checked with Bunty who said she had missed him by only minutes and that he had seemed in fine form. He had mellowed, she felt, which was not before time. Once he'd come over as condescending, as though he had done their daughter a favour by bedding her in her teens. Now, however, he showed more respect, asked thoughtful questions about the shop; had even admired the hats they were making which he had judged first-rate.

'He especially liked the one you tried on. Agreed it would be perfect for you. Who knows, you may still get one as a surprise.'

Bunty might laugh but Rose did not. Her lip was curling with rage. How dare they discuss her behind her back. She remembered Lily's disdainful remark. Whatever it took she would find a way to end the marriage and get Joe back. First, however, she had to deal with Sukey.

Sukey lived in Colliers Wood where she shared a house with a couple of nurses, both currently on vacation. It wasn't too hard to find her; Rose had Ann to thank though did what she could to cover her tracks by letting her think it was Lily who wanted to know. Ann's mean little eyes really glowed with delight, loving to think that the wife was now in on the act. But word must not get out, urged Rose. Or else she would have betrayed her sister.

Ann took the bait like a seasoned piranha and soon had details of everyone's movements. On Saturdays, between twelve and six, Sukey manned the department's emergency line. She would, therefore, almost certainly be at home.

'You are sure of that?'

'She is on the rota.' Ann was wasted in the civil service, should transfer to MI5.

'How do you know?'

'I searched her desk.' The blackcurrant eyes were alive with malice. Her favourite occupation was wreaking harm.

'And left no traces?'

'I'm not a fool.' The Asian bitch had it coming to her. Had been putting it out all over the place, so she'd heard.

Joe was due to speak in Strasbourg, addressing the European Parliament on the uses of nuclear physics against global warming. Lily was taking advantage of his absence to visit an IVF clinic. She wanted to keep it confidential until she knew what her chances were. She didn't want him disappointed again.

No problem, they said. It was up to her. As a private patient, no questions would be asked. They referred her to a male consultant. Dr Buchan, they told her, was one of the best. He was young and extremely well qualified. They asked for a sample of her blood as well as payment in cash. Lily, excited, told Bunty and Rose but asked them to keep it from her father. She didn't want to raise false expectations.

Rather than drive, Rose took the tube, not wanting to risk her number plate's being caught by CCTV. She turned up the collar of her raincoat and swapped her lenses for National Health glasses. She carried a brief-case containing a clipboard in case she was asked who she was.

35

The house was scruffy, with dustbins outside. There was no one around in the street. When Sukey opened the door, she seemed taken aback.

'Rose,' she said, after a fleeting pause while she obviously struggled to place the face. 'What are you doing in these parts? Come in.'

She was wearing leggings and a paint-splashed T-shirt. Small and flat-chested, she was exquisite, with the face of a porcelain doll.

'We need to talk.' Rose swept inside, dropping the briefcase on to a chair but keeping her raincoat on and firmly belted. She stood in the hall and looked around; the house was in need of some urgent work.

'I'm painting the living room,' Sukey said, obviously reading her mind.

She led Rose into the kitchen instead which was

overcrowded with too many chairs. The sink was piled high with unwashed dishes. She's also a slut, thought Rose.

Sukey switched on the kettle and offered her tea. Rose said she wouldn't be staying long.

'I was in the area,' she lied, 'and wanted a private word.'

Sukey shifted the dishes from the sink in order to scrub her hands. Her neat little oval nails were rimmed with paint. Masking tape and a jumble of brushes were strewn on the newspaper-covered table. The place stank of paint and turpentine, a combination that almost made Rose gag.

Having cleaned off the paint and dried her hands, Sukey offered Rose one of the chairs, then perched like a robin on the edge of the table, politely waiting to hear what she had to say.

'Where are your flatmates?' Rose had to be sure.

'In Austria, skiing,' said Sukey.

'So you're here alone?'

'I am,' she said. 'Trust them to push off and leave me to fix up the place.' Since, however, she was on call it wasn't too much of a hardship.

'I need to talk to you about Joe.' Restlessly Rose began to pace. The girl had the gall to show no sign of contrition.

Sukey said nothing, just cocked her head, her

expression entirely impassive. She didn't appear to be alarmed or, for that matter, evasive.

'Your boss is my sister's husband,' said Rose. 'And I can't have you wrecking her marriage. Everyone knows you've been carrying on so don't even try to deny it.'

Sukey's expression scarcely flickered. 'I have no idea what you mean,' she said.

'It's common knowledge in Westminster. You've not had the manners to cover your tracks. Joe is a very distinguished man whereas you're no more than a slut.'

She hadn't intended to lose control but this flash of rage tipped her over the edge. Her eyes raked the overcrowded room for a way of silencing the strumpet. 'I've changed my mind,' she said. 'I would like that tea.'

It was true what they said; they *were* inscrutable. Without reacting, Sukey slipped off the table and went to do Rose's bidding.

'You're making a dreadful mistake,' she said as she boiled the water and rinsed out mugs. 'We are nothing more to each other than boss and PA.'

'Rubbish!' said Rose, really losing control and reaching for the masking tape. Though slight herself she was bigger than Sukey who had the physique of a nine-year-old child who might snap in two like a twig. It shouldn't be hard; she had silenced her brother when he'd got in her way at the age of two. She closed in on Sukey and grabbed her throat; the girl fought like a panicking cat. But Rose was stronger; she seized both her arms, twisting them back and securing her wrists with the tape. She hefted her, kicking and screaming, to a chair and plonked her there while she hurled abuse. Any attempt at restraint was entirely lost.

'Please,' screamed Sukey, 'you've got it wrong. I like him a lot but don't fancy him. Apart from anything else, he is much too old.'

Rose, now completely out of control, slapped her hard across both cheeks. 'Bitch!' she screeched. 'Don't speak of him in that way.'

Using J-cloths to secure Sukey's legs, she gagged her tightly with masking tape then seated herself in the other girl's place, on the edge of the table, glaring down. She certainly had her full attention.

'Now listen here and listen good.' Rose again had the upper hand. 'Joe Markovich belongs to me. Let nobody ever forget that.'

Sukey's beautiful almond-shaped eyes were wide with alarm though she couldn't speak. She had stopped attempting to flail her legs, aware that it would be futile. Rose, recalling the Garbo hat, observed how striking the girl truly was. Early twenties, as frail as a bird, transfixed now by total fear. She indicated that she wished to speak; Rose laughed and lit a cigarette. The pressure was off; she had plenty of time to achieve what she'd set out to do.

The doorbell rang and both girls froze.

'Are you expecting someone?' Rose asked.

Sukey mutely shook her head. The eyes above the gag were wild and imploring.

Rose stepped into the hall and listened. A leaflet came fluttering through the door. The local council elections; she relaxed.

'He's mine,' she repeated, one hand in her pocket. 'I am going to ensure that you never see him again.'

A crafty smile crept on to her face; her eyes were narrow and gleaming. She produced from her pocket a pair of surgical gloves. She held the hatpin cupped in her palm, triumphant that she had thought to bring it. She brought her face up close to Sukey's, watching the terror in her eyes. Those beautiful eyes that had seen too much. She raised her hand and, swift as a cobra, struck.

The final touch was pure genius. Rose peeled off the gloves and went upstairs to check out her hair and face and if there was blood. The bathroom was as cluttered as Lily's, with underwear drying over the tub and a jumble of makeup on the shelf by the basin. She felt in her pocket and found the lipstick, the one she had filched from her sister's flat which, knowing Lily, would probably never be missed. Replacing the gloves, she wiped it clean to make extra sure that she hadn't left prints, then placed it among the rest of the stuff on the shelf.

Sooner or later the police would find it. She wasn't in any hurry.

36

News of Sukey's macabre death hit the media on Monday night in a very major way. She hadn't been fielding department calls and, when she failed to turn up for work, somebody went to the house. Lily phoned Rose in a state of shock. The police had met Joe off his afternoon flight and taken him in for questioning.

Rose was appalled. 'Why on earth?' she asked. The thought had never occurred to her.

'It's purely routine, or so they said. But someone who claims to know has been spreading rumours. About him and Sukey.'

'But surely he has an alibi.' She was practically speechless; her plan had misfired.

'So I would have thought,' said Lily, 'but he's been away for several days so they have to trace his movements.'

Matthew wanted to come and fetch her but Lily

refused to leave the flat until she knew for certain Joe was all right. Instead Rose packed an overnight bag and went straight over to hold her hand. That's what elder sisters were for and she was as keen as Lily to know he was safe.

'You don't really think it is true after all?' Lily was almost speechless with fright. 'That he was having it off with her? If he was, I won't forgive him.'

'No,' said Rose, who was equally shocked. This was not how things were supposed to have gone. She had a bone to pick with Ann who had grossly overreacted.

'Why would he kill her?'

'He won't have done. She must have had somebody else in her life. Or else it was simply a random break-in. She lived in a dodgy part of town.'

'How do you know?'

'I read it,' said Rose, annoyed with herself for letting it slip. She must pull herself together and try to think calmly. There had been no witnesses to the crime; the flatmates were gone and no one had come to the house. Except for whoever it was who'd delivered the leaflet. Sukey had been on call but the phone hadn't rung. And Rose had carefully worn disguise. The first thing she'd do, once she left this flat, was drop the NHS spectacles down a drain. She'd already carefully hidden the hatpin where, with luck, it would be eventually found.

'Suppose he did do it.' Lily was shaking, the baby blue eyes filled with terrible fear.

'Don't be absurd,' snapped Rose. 'He couldn't have done.' This was the man she had always adored, whose reputation she'd defend with her life. Events might have taken a slightly wrong turn but would, in the end, work out.

She poured Lily a brandy and they watched the news. She must keep a clear head so did not drink herself. There were photos of Sukey at her glamorous best. A man was helping with inquiries, the newscaster said. Then there was Ann, with her boot-button eyes and an ill-concealed smile on her satisfied face. She wasn't at all surprised, she said. There had been a lot of talk.

'Bitch!' said Rose, who had egged her on. Providing Joe could clear himself, this might work out, after all, the way she had planned.

She offered to cook them scrambled eggs but Lily had lost her appetite so instead Rose topped up her glass and made herself coffee. They watched as much news as they could find, then Matthew called to check how they were and Bunty came on the phone and cried a lot.

'Pull yourself together,' said Rose. 'It won't help Lily if you crack up.'

'Do you think he did it?' her mother whispered.

'No,' said Rose. 'I do not.'

She instructed them both to get off the phone in case the police were trying to reach them. Sooner or later the press would track them down.

'If you want me, I'll come,' her father said.

She told him to stay home and take care of Bunty.

It was midnight before they heard Joe's key. They were huddled together beneath a rug and Lily had cried herself out. She had run it all through any number of times till Rose was attempting to close her mind. She knew he'd be able to clear himself but couldn't convince her sister.

'Why not go to bed?' she suggested. 'I'll wait up till there's news.'

'No,' said Lily, still distraught. She knew she would never sleep.

And then he came in and his face was grim. He suddenly looked about ten years older. He clasped his wife in his arms until she stopped crying. 'It's all right,' he said gently, stroking her hair, and Rose remembered, in a vivid flashback, the night he had caught her when she toppled from the tree. They looked at each other with the same rapt gaze; something within her jerked and spat. She had gone to such lengths to split them up; could not have them reconciled now.

How did things go?' She controlled herself and poured him a glass of bourbon. 'I bet you feel like this,' she said.

'I certainly do,' he replied, still hugging his wife.

He sat on the sofa and mopped his face and Lily, childlike, snuggled beside him. He absent-mindedly stroked her shoulder but, for a while, didn't speak.

At last he looked up and his eyes were raw. 'It was unbelievably awful,' he said.

Slowly, in carefully chosen words, he explained what appeared to have happened to Sukey. 'They had to take me in,' he said. 'As part of routine procedure.'

'What was so awful?' She had to find out just how much the police had deduced. She must be exceedingly careful now not to give herself away.

He closed his eyes at the memory. 'Some maniac seems to have broken in and caught her alone, with both her flatmates away.'

'What did he do?' It was Lily who asked.

'Believe me, you really don't want to know.' Just thinking about the path lab's pictures almost made him throw up. 'I can only say that whoever it was has to be totally raving mad. To do a thing like that with such precision.'

'So why were you ever in the frame?'

'I told you. Purely routine.' He had proof he had been where he'd said at the time; five hundred delegates had heard him speak and snatches of his talk had been televised.

'Thank God,' breathed Lily, snuggling closer and

pressing her face against his chest. Rose itched to tear them apart but controlled herself.

It was late so all three of them went to bed and when Rose emerged, he'd already left. For the present the police had let him go but he could not leave the country. They had his passport.

'Do you believe him?' asked Lily quietly.

'Of course,' snapped Rose. 'Don't you?'

The minute Rose arrived at work, Ann was there, positively gloating.

'Whoever would have thought it,' she said. 'Your little sister seems so demure. It's amazing what a woman will do when she catches her husband cheating.'

Rose, enraged, simply froze her out. 'Mind your own damn business,' she said. Having so carefully set a false trail, she now had the delicate task of controlling Ann. Just enough gossip but not too much; in no way must she appear complicit. She needed to draw a very fine line if her master plan were to work.

She withdrew to her office and closed the door. There were piles of urgent messages waiting, mainly from the press and police and Esther who'd called three times. The others would have to wait while she called her back.

* * *

Esther spoke in a scandalised whisper. 'Now what have you been up to?' she said. She knew Rose too well to believe that she wasn't involved, though the thought appalled her.

'I've no idea what you mean,' said Rose, trying her hardest to fob Esther off, knowing her greatest danger lay with this friend who could read her so well. Though would never betray her, of that she was sure. The friendship they'd had all their lives went far too deep.

'Don't tell me it was coincidence. Things don't happen as neatly as that. It does seem oddly convenient that Sukey should die.'

'Dreadful,' said Rose. 'I entirely agree. Poor Joe, the police have been on his case. Thank God, he has a watertight alibi.'

Esther sighed. 'Just watch your step.' She knew Rose too well to be taken in; also how ruthless she might be should anyone stand in her way.

'Why do you still defend her?' asked Meg, who had always been wary of Rose. Esther was saintly in the extreme but this time was turning too blind an eye. 'You have to tell the police,' Meg said. 'Or at least alert someone else to what's going on.'

'I can't,' said Esther. 'You don't understand. We've relied on each other for most of our lives.' Since their first day at school. She remembered it well, herself a clumsy and overweight child with bottle lenses and frizzy hair, the laughing stock of the class. Rose had been elegant and petite with a sharp intelligence that dazzled them all. For whatever reason, she'd befriended Esther, perhaps because, deep down, they were both misfits. They had instantly bonded. Rose had taught her chess and they'd stuck together through thick and thin. Till Oxford, when Esther came into her own and Rose had fatally fallen for that jerk.

'In what way is he bad?' asked Meg who had only seen Joe on television. A greying boffin with a ponderous manner; not her idea of a heart-throb.

'It's not so much him as her,' Esther said. 'She misinterpreted how he felt and he, for whatever reason, led her on.' Not the thing to do with Rose whose connection with reality was always shaky. Something to do with her blinkered vision because she was so bright.

'But you can't let her get away with it. She is verging now on the dangerous. If she had anything to do with Sukey's murder, you know it's your duty to shop her.'

'I can't,' said Esther with stricken eyes. 'I have no proof. She is far too smart. And needs me around to keep her sane. She is balancing on a knife edge.'

'Why?' asked Meg, now angry and jealous.

'Because I'm her only friend.'

37

Suddenly Lily and Joe appeared closer, almost an echo of what they had been. To Rose it was incomprehensible though Matthew and Bunty were pleased.

'She's been through such a terrible time. The murder was almost too much to bear. And Joe, poor Joe, went through even worse. Is still officially on the list of suspects.'

The case was still hanging fire in the press; if there were leads, they had not been revealed. The papers had raked through Sukey's past but not, as far as anyone knew, come up with anything special. Ann still had that knowing look which Rose did her best to ignore. She must not be seen to have any connection with the rumours. The flatmates had cut their holiday short and been summoned home to assist inquiries. Both were predictably traumatised yet unable to throw any light on the case. Sukey and Joe had worked closely together but only in a professional sense. Neither girl, separately interviewed, admitted to even having met him. He was too high profile for there not to be gossip but, due to absence of evidence, it rapidly started to fade.

Soon, of course, they came after Lily; she was next in line to be interviewed. They were deferential and kept it brief but needed to know her movements that afternoon.

'It's normal procedure,' they explained, the detectives who came to check her out. Could she confirm what she had been doing? And had she personally known the murdered woman?

'Only in passing,' said Lily vaguely. Sukey had once or twice been to the flat but only ever in the course of doing her job. 'My husband thought her a very good worker. I know nothing about her private life.' She didn't repeat what she'd said to Rose, that she'd found her a bit of a crawler.

And where had she been that day? they repeated. Lily knew precisely but scratched her head. It was none of their damn business, she wanted to say.

'A consultation with a doctor,' she said, enraged that they had the nerve to insist. 'I'd prefer that you keep that confidential. I don't want my husband to know.'

She saw the significant glance they exchanged and cursed herself for her stupidity. 'If you want to check it out,' she said, 'you can have his private number.'

The cops might be satisfied. Bunty was not. She wanted to know in minute detail what Dr Buchan had said.

Lily softened. 'It's not too late.' He had done a series of medical tests as well as monitored her hormone level. 'My Fallopian tubes are both infected which is why I haven't conceived before now. But he thinks the situation can be reversed.'

They hugged each other and shrieked with joy. 'He told me to take things easy,' said Lily. 'If only this wretched business would go away.'

If Lily was happy, Rose was not though she kept her feelings carefully in check. She avoided Esther like the plague, unwilling to face her constant probing questions. Whatever she guessed, she could not be sure and Rose would never confide in her. From this point on she was on her own. She was glad that Hugo was not still around.

Meanwhile, the lovebirds – as Matthew now dubbed them – had reached a new level of connubial bliss. The total awfulness of the crime seemed to have jolted Joe's indifference. He might, or might not, have been Sukey's lover but he'd never forget her horrible death. He started coming home on time and got the piano out of storage. He was even civil to Rose whenever she phoned.

'Are you sure he's not covering something up?' Ann asked the question which Rose ignored although she no longer shouted her down. She mustn't allow the rumours to die altogether.

'Leave me alone,' was all she'd say. 'I've enough on my plate with my sister acting oddly.'

The police had gone unnervingly quiet. They surely couldn't just leave it like that. Sukey's murder was a nine days' wonder; other equally lurid stories elbowed her off the front page.

And then, one morning in the early hours, Rose was woken by a call from Joe, sounding confused and not a little distraught. The police had been and arrested Lily. He found it hard to get out the words.

'For what?' asked Rose, quickly gathering her wits. At the sound of his voice she was suddenly fully awake.

'For Sukey's murder,' he said. 'I can't take it in.'

She closed her eyes in silent prayer. Finally a result, she breathed. 'I'll be over right away,' she said. 'Do nothing until I get there.'

He'd had time to dress but hadn't shaved. He looked alarmed and wild-eyed. Rose went and put her arms round him and held him tight in a sisterly hug.

'Come and I'll make coffee,' she said. 'Have you told my parents?'

He shook his head; there hadn't been time and he'd

wanted to wait until Rose was there. He still didn't quite understand the implications.

'Lily?' said Rose with an inner glow, efficiently heating the coffee pot. 'How did they come to such an unlikely conclusion?'

Joe didn't know. They had both been asleep. He hadn't heard all the evidence yet, only that they'd located the murder weapon. An antique hatpin, eight inches long; it must have fallen when they moved the body. They had proved that it came from Lily's workroom. She had used it to penetrate both Sukey's eyes then driven it into her brain.

'Gruesome,' said Rose, stirring in extra sugar. 'But how come it wasn't discovered before? It must have been on the murder scene all the time.'

'The ambulance men were very young. It is thought that one of them fainted,' said Joe. Having seen pictures of what they had found, he wasn't remotely surprised.

'So how do they know it belonged to Lily?'

'It came from her workroom,' he said. 'Now that I know, I remember it well. She used it in her shows.'

They sat in silence and drank their coffee, their minds both set on different things. Thank God they finally found it, thought Rose. She had hidden it where it would be initially unobserved but the fact they had taken so long had begun to unnerve her.

'I can't believe she did it,' said Joe. 'There isn't a

spark of malice in her.' His striking face with its brooding eyes looked even more hangdog than usual.

Damn it, thought Rose, in a flash of rage. I do believe he loves her.

In due course they summoned Matthew and Bunty who got there in record time. Bunty rushed in and threw herself into Joe's arms.

'My darling child. Where is she?' she asked. 'She needs me with her, I know she does.' She hadn't even stopped to put on makeup.

Typical overreaction, Rose thought sourly.

Matthew told them all to calm down though he looked as if he might have a stroke himself. The thought of his baby girl in jail was more than he could take in. Joe, now fully back in control – he had even shaved before they arrived – took formal charge of the proceedings, master, once more, in his own home.

'It's a great miscarriage of justice,' he said. 'We all know Lily couldn't hurt a fly, nor did she have motivation. It doesn't add up.'

Whereupon, on cue, the telephone rang. A policeman, asking to speak to him. Lily was to be formally charged. They'd identified her DNA on a lipstick in Sukey's bathroom.

38

She looked such a sad little scrap of a thing when she finally came into court. The bloom had entirely gone from her cheeks and the glorious hair was now matted and dull. She wore an ill-fitting prison garment in an unflattering shade of grey. From the gallery Bunty gave a loud sob and Matthew turned visibly paler. Rose instinctively gripped Joe's hand. Since Lily's arrest they had grown considerably closer.

She was charged, said the judge, with the savage murder of Sukey Khan of Colliers Wood, whose eyes she had gouged out with a lethal weapon. What was her response to the charge?

'Not guilty,' she said in the faintest whisper. The onlookers had to crane forward to catch it at all.

The Prosecution, who was suave and glib, proceeded then to describe the crime, portraying Lily as a frenzied killer who had stabbed an innocent girl to death solely from motives of vengeance.

'Objection!' Defence Counsel leapt to her feet; Bunty was glad they had chosen a woman. 'She believed the victim to be having relations with her husband, Joseph Markovich. The crime, if there was one, was a plea for help at a time when she was slightly unbalanced, fearing the imminent break-up of her marriage.'

'I didn't do it.' That was Lily again but no one by now was listening to her. All eyes, instead, were on the gallery where Joe, grim-faced, sat surrounded by Prescotts, as public a statement as he could make that he hadn't lost faith in his wife. Bunty, broken, was audibly weeping and had to be cautioned by the judge for causing a disturbance in court. Matthew wrapped his arm round her and held her tightly against his chest. As tightly as Rose was clinging to Joe's hand.

The Prosecution was back on his feet. The evidence was conclusive, he said. Her fingerprints had been found on the weapon and a lipstick in the victim's house bore traces of Lily's DNA.

'Objection,' cried Defence Counsel again. The fact she had been in the victim's house proved only that they were acquainted which, since the victim had worked for her husband, was not altogether surprising. They were women of a similar age. There was no reason, surely, why they shouldn't be friends.

The Prosecution was smiling now. Did it seem likely,

he asked the jury, that a wife whose husband was flagrantly unfaithful should cosy up to his bit on the side? Unless, of course, she had a more sinister motive.

'Order,' thumped the judge, not liking his choice of words.

As well as a plea of crime passionnel, the Defence was giving it all she had got; Lily was ordered to be detained until the second hearing in two weeks' time. They took her away, with eyes downcast, looking so frail she could hardly stand. Joe, with her family still at his side, led the way out through a thicket of flash-bulbs.

'What have you to say?' roared the press.

He acted as though he hadn't heard.

The summing up went straight to the point. The motive was there; the accused had no real defence. Her position was not improved by Ann, who'd contrived to worm her way on to the stand and had her fifteen minutes of fame denouncing poor innocent Lily. In her own distinctly clichéd way, she said there was never smoke without fire, flashing her mean little eyes at the jury, assuming they would believe her. Joe, she told them, was a practised seducer who had married his much younger wife as soon as she came of age.

'What has she got against him?' asked Bunty. 'What harm has he ever done to her?' Though she had once had serious doubts, she was now firmly on Joe's side. He had shown himself to be a dependable husband.

'Nothing,' said Rose. 'Which is mainly the point. Ann can't abide being ignored.'

She could scarcely believe things were going so well. Proceedings were likely to wind up soon. The fact that it was her sister up there in no way troubled her conscience. At least, these days, they no longer hanged them; with luck she'd get remission if she behaved. Lily's future was incidental; the crucial thing for Rose was time in which to make Joe understand that they should now be together. Part of her wished the court had called her. She saw herself wearing the Garbo hat, publicly pleading for Lily's freedom while, simultaneously, digging her in even deeper.

Lily was taking it all very badly; proceedings had to be halted twice because she was feeling unwell.

'She's putting it on, just playing for time,' said someone seated directly behind them and Rose turned fiercely and ordered him to shut up.

'Silence,' thundered the judge again, 'or else I will clear the court.'

The sticking point was the alibi; Lily didn't have one. She claimed she'd had a doctor's appointment on the afternoon of Sukey's murder, though hadn't told her husband about it because it was confidential. Up in the gallery, Joe looked surprised; Rose was clocking his every expression. She still hadn't told him, silly girl, and now her story would never hold up. What sort of wife deceives her husband about such a sensitive thing?

Lily, terrified, talked to her counsel who sent her clerk to investigate. True to their word, the private clinic claimed no knowledge of Lily's having been there. She had checked in under a pseudonym since her married name was so well known. She hadn't wanted to let Joe down. If he didn't know he could not be disappointed.

The police interviewed the receptionist too and confiscated the register. Lily, having never had very much imagination, had used a name she had heard her sister mention more than once.

'There I am.' She pointed out *Ann Cole* though had no way of proving it had been her. The only person she'd seen that day, apart from the temporary nursing staff, had been the glamorous climbing-mad consultant. Thus she was one of the first to find out that the man in whose hands her alibi lay had tragically died in an accident at the weekend.

No confirmation; no alibi. Which, combined with the prints and the DNA, was all the Prosecution needed. In all, the proceedings were shockingly brief. The jury voted as one to find Lily guilty. Guilty of murdering a rival in love in the most barbaric and repulsive way the judge, in all his years, had ever encountered. After he had conferred with both lawyers, Lily was sentenced to fifteen years, lighter than it might have been since her counsel convinced the judge she was not compos mentis at the time. They led her away, like a broken doll, to incarceration in Holloway jail and Bunty broke down and cried so much the paramedics were called.

Rose stood silently at Joe's side, relieved it had all worked out so well and the obstacle to her dreams had at last been removed. For seven years she had lived in hell. Now, at last, she saw light at the end of the tunnel.

The story was barely off the front page, and the Prescotts had yet to adjust to the outcome, when Lily tossed another grenade that no one had foreseen. Against all odds, she was pregnant at last, even without any IVF. Nature had finally taken its course, perhaps because she'd had other things on her mind. The baby was due in seven months. It would, alas, be born behind bars. They would lodge a plea for a shortened sentence but there wasn't much likelihood it would work. The savagery of the crime went very much against her.

After the initial shock, when they didn't know

whether to laugh or cry, Matthew and Bunty admitted to having mixed feelings. What kind of future could any child have whose mother was a convicted killer? They might well have to raise it themselves since the father seemed in denial. But at least it gave Lily's life some purpose, the one thing she'd longed for for so many years. And they could provide a discreet and stable background. Bunty immediately thought of Simon. She prayed Lily's baby would be a boy. This time round she would be more careful and never let him out of her sight, at least until she was satisfied he could swim.

'You can't allow her to keep it,' said Rose. It seemed that Lily had won again.

'We'll raise him as our own,' said Bunty 'until poor Lily is back on her feet.' Whether or not it could save the marriage, only time would tell.

39

When Lily's time came they shifted her into the prison's hospital wing where the only visitor she was allowed was her husband. Bunty wanted to go along too but rules were rules and Lily was classified as dangerous. She didn't look it when Joe came in, slumped in front of the television in fluffy slippers and clutching a teddy bear. Joe could find nothing to say to her. She looked at him with great saucer eyes, as guilelessly innocent as she had been the very first time they had met.

'How are you feeling?'

'It's started.' She wore her dressing gown undone and her prison robe stretched tightly over her knees. The mound that was his son or daughter made Joe inwardly shudder. He wasn't ready to face the extra commitment.

'When will they come to take you away?'

'Any time now,' she said.

He had brought her flowers which he laid on the bed. She nodded a lustreless thank you. He pulled up the only chair and sat beside her.

Her skin was clammy when he touched her wrist; there were purple shadows beneath her eyes. She was certainly not the picture of health; he wondered if that was normal.

'What do the doctors say?' he asked.

'They mutter among themselves,' she said. 'I don't imagine they care either way what happens to patients in here.' She gave a dry little rusty cough and laughed.

Joe slid over to sit on the bed, moving the flowers to a safer place. Her belly was huge but her face looked positively haggard.

He stroked her hair. 'I'm so sorry,' he said.

'For what?' she asked him searchingly. In that fleeting second, he saw the hope die in her eyes.

'For landing you in this terrible mess.' He instinctively reached for a cigarette then remembered, in time, where he was; that it wasn't allowed.

'It wasn't your fault. I was careless,' she said. Her matter-of-factness alarmed him. 'I wanted so badly to have your child. I would have done whatever it took. I wish I hadn't lied to you. If I'd told you, I wouldn't be in here.'

Joe was extremely uncomfortable. He was still

confused about how he felt. She seemed so helpless yet, at the same time, in control.

'But you didn't do it?'

'Of course not,' she said. 'Do you really know me as little as that?' And then she started convulsions and couldn't stop.

'What should I do?' He felt such a fool, the world famous scientist unable to cope in a domestic situation like this. She was choking now and her face was turning blue.

'Call them,' she gasped, indicating the alarm. He did as she said and yanked at the cord. In a matter of seconds came the sound of running feet and the medical staff took over. They rolled Lily deftly on to a trolley and indicated that Joe should leave.

'Wait in reception,' an orderly said. 'We'll call you when there's news.'

He stood in the doorway to whisper goodbye.

'Did you ever love me?' she gasped. Her eyes were huge and cornflower blue. She was so much like that enchanting child, he thought his heart might break. He stretched out his hand but couldn't quite reach.

'Don't be absurd,' he said.

Rose taxied over to sit with Joe; he was too unsettled to be alone which, when she phoned to find out about Lily, she instantly picked up.

'I'll cook for you.'

'Don't bother,' he said. He'd encountered her somewhat inept attempts and, in any case, had no appetite. He was too strung up about Lily.

She would come in any case, Rose said. 'Perhaps we should go to the pub.' But Joe pointed out that he had to stay close to the phone.

'You could always use your mobile,' she said. He reminded her it was not a private clinic but a prison.

He opened a bottle of very good wine.

'To wet the baby's head,' she said but Joe was tense and preoccupied, not in a party mood. There was something about Lily's final words that struck him with a dark foreboding. Had he loved her? He now wasn't sure. It was seven years and he only vaguely remembered. He had lusted after her at the start, knocked out by her dazzling and innocent beauty and the childlike element that made him want to protect her. She wasn't clever, not like Rose, but shared her mother's simplicity. As a wife she'd left much to be desired though had the knack of making him laugh. And he'd always been proud to be seen with her. Affection, yes, but not love, he now realised.

Rose sat and watched him silently brooding and her heart brimmed over with such fierce emotion, she could scarcely stop herself falling prone at his feet. It was sixteen years since that moment at Rick's when she'd first been electrified by Joe's playing and over-whelmed by a passion so strong she had never since looked at another man, not in more than a faint incurious way. She would never know why he'd chosen her sister when she was so obviously wrong for him. To this day she blamed Lily for totally wrecking her life.

No, not love, he was ruminating. Love was an altogether stronger emotion. Love was what Matthew and Bunty shared in their offbeat, apparently mismatched way. Though Matthew said little and was often gruff, sunk in his paper while listening to music or shut in his study, perfecting plans, he occasionally stole a covert glance that betrayed how he still felt. On the surface they seemed to have little in common; she wittered on while he was a man of few words. He read *The Times*, she the *Daily Mail*; he watched the news and she the soaps, they went to bed at different times and she struggled up to make his breakfast during which he rarely spoke. And yet there was an unbroken cord; he was there for her when her heart was breaking, like now when she watched her beloved daughter enduring pain over which she had no control. That was love of the purest kind. What the much missed Jean-Paul had shared with his Annette.

The telephone rang and he leapt up, deliberately closing the door so that Rose couldn't hear. She topped up her glass and strained her ears but his voice was low and gave nothing away. She used his absence to smooth down her hair and rapidly touch up her makeup. Until Joe Markovich entered her life, vanity had been alien to her. She had grown up indifferent to how she looked, having shared her life with a Barbie doll mother and a sister who was Bunty's clone. She had closed her mind to their endless chatter, the perusal of fashions in magazines. She focused her not inconsiderable brain on passing exams and playing chess or figuring out the intricacies of Bach and the universe. Until she'd seen Joe and her axis had changed. Rose had descended from her peak and become a needy woman.

His voice had stopped. She resumed her seat, crossing her legs and smoothing her skirt, and picked up the paper, pretending she hadn't been listening.

He stood in the doorway. His expression was bleak. 'They need me there. It is not looking good.'

'Wait while I get my coat,' she said and followed him out to the car.

Things looked grave. There was something wrong. The baby was not responding as well as it should. She had been in labour a full eight hours and was losing a great deal of blood. Matthew and Bunty sat close to the phone, Joe having promised to call when he could.

Both were shaking and pale with shock; they had been through too much already.

'Was it our fault?' Matthew wanted to know. 'Letting her marry a much older man?'

'We couldn't have stopped her,' Bunty said. 'I told you that at the time.'

Rose was there with Joe, he had said, which did seem strange when they thought about it. It was not like her to be so concerned, especially when it was Lily in trouble. Relations between the sisters were still very strained.

'I don't believe Rose will ever forgive her for stealing the one great love of her life.'

Matthew, who'd put it out of his mind, looked surprised. 'Rose and Joe? Oh, come now,' he said. 'It was never more than a passing crush. Her first romance as a kid at Oxford which never amounted to much.'

'More than you think,' hinted Bunty darkly. 'Your older daughter has hidden depths.' Lily changed boyfriends as often as she had herself until she had married at twenty-two and devoted the rest of her life to her husband and children. Lily had never been happy with Joe, not once the romance had started to fade. She had rapidly tired of the role she had chosen, the infant bride of a highly intelligent man.

Lily had found that she couldn't compete. Just being pretty was not enough. In some ways Bunty had felt the same though, in her case, her husband had always loved her. Not that it often showed, of course. He was adept at hiding his feelings, like Rose. Now he was still looking faintly stunned.

'Rose and Joe?' he repeated.

'You knew that,' said Bunty. 'You've just forgotten. That night when he came to the house when Lily was a child.' It had happened then; she saw that now. Their coming together had been forestalled by the fact that Lily had needed another nine years in which to grow up. And poor old Rose had been sacrificed. Despite her talent and brilliant mind, she was human, just like the rest of them, with powerful feelings she'd managed to hide from her father.

There were times when men could be so obtuse. The telephone rang; Matthew answered it.

'You had best come quickly.' Joe's voice was thick. 'Lily has taken a sudden turn for the worse.'

Rose had stepped out for a cigarette when a nurse appeared and beckoned to her.

'Where are the parents?' she asked.

'They are on their way.'

'Better come in and take their place. She needs her family round her now.' The woman's habitually sour expression had switched to one of concern.

Rose stamped on her butt end and followed her in.

Her pulse raced with suppressed excitement. Something monumental was happening; she was glad to be in at the kill.

Joe was wearing a surgeon's smock and holding a tiny white-blanketed bundle. His eyes were moist when he turned to Rose and placed it gently in her arms.

'Meet your niece, Daisy,' he said to her gruffly before re-joining the group round the bed where the doctors were doing their utmost to save the patient.

Her niece. Rose cradled the fragile creature, too young yet to show any animate signs. Her flesh and blood but also Joe's. Another extraordinary twist of fate had drawn them still closer together.

Bunty and Matthew burst into the room. Too late, for Lily was dead.

Part Three

40

With Lily's death, the Prescott family began perceptibly to unravel. The glue that had held them together had lost its grip. The dreadful events had shattered both parents though Rose took a more philosophical stance, surprising them with her endless concern for the baby. Joe seemed out of it, lost and withdrawn, existing alone on a separate planet, heedless of the needs of his infant daughter. So Rose stepped in with her management skills and took it upon herself to sort things out. Which was as well, with Bunty failing, back in the tortured night of the soul she had experienced before when she lost her son. Matthew, also, was not in good shape. His breathing had become heavy and laboured and his face took on the texture and colour of putty. Rose suggested he see a doctor but he told her she was making a fuss. What a bunch of walking wounded they were. Rose was not emotionally equipped to empathise with their raw and continuing grief. Neither did she give them much thought, her one-track mind being focused on other things.

Lily's death had opened a door. She saw her chance and was instantly in there. Joe was clearly a broken man, consumed by guilt at Lily's fate which he felt he should have been able to prevent.

'She didn't do it. She can't have done. There wasn't an ounce of evil in her. If I'd paid more attention I might have prevented it happening.'

With his head in his hands, he rocked in sorrow while Rose contrived never to leave his side. Without invitation or even discussion, she had moved into his spare room. They were family now. No one, she felt, had more right.

'You can't look after that baby alone.' Esther thoroughly disapproved, knowing Rose too well to be taken in.

'She's my niece,' said Rose, as she rocked the cradle. Joe's daughter was what she really meant and, if it were to bring them closer, there was nothing she wouldn't do.

'A baby that age needs a full-time carer.'

The auxiliaries, meanwhile, were standing in. Joe was unwilling to put Daisy in care and Bunty, quite simply, couldn't cope. Esther sighed; Rose was at it again. Who knew what damage she yet might wreak.

But she'd learnt long ago not to interfere when Rose was working to a private agenda.

A nursery maid was what was called for; there was room in the flat for one living in. Rose interviewed a succession of girls, looking for someone she could control who would not intrude on Joe's privacy or play too central a role. Rose with a baby – whatever next? If it weren't so tragic the concept was comic. Though having a minder living in meant Rose must relinquish her room.

The police inquiry died with Lily. They had nailed their killer and closed the case. Rose discreetly sold the shop, helping herself to the Garbo hat as a symbol of how her fortunes seemed to be changing. Instead of lingering late in the office, disinclined to return to her sterile flat, she now left promptly on the stroke of six to rush to Joe's place ahead of him and get a meal on the table. After they'd eaten she would linger on, clearing the dishes and tidying up. She took on duties that once were Lily's, even cleaning the bathrooms and changing the sheets.

'You really don't have to do that,' said Joe, too dispirited to argue much.

'You're turning into a right little skivvy.' Ann, with her sneers, was still on his case. Her moment of fame had faded fast and nobody talked to her any more.

Rightly or wrongly, she was perceived as a traitor. What she'd done to Lily had shocked them all; the department, as one, shut her out. Rose, conversely, gained brownie points for so valiantly leaping to the widower's aid. Few women as ambitious as her would risk it all for a motherless niece. Despite the image that Rose projected, it appeared that she must, after all, possess a heart.

Joe came later and later home, absorbed once more by his government job. His initial contract was just for one year and would soon be due for renewal. No problem there, Rose was satisfied. In the circles that counted he was held in the highest esteem. His input to the environmental issue, she knew from Esther, had been noted at the top. There was little question that he'd be invited to stay on.

'He's not going to leave us?' Matthew was anxious, could not bear Bunty to suffer more pain. The loss of Lily had almost destroyed her. To lose her grand-daughter too might finish her off.

'Of course he'll stay. We're his family now. Besides, where else is he likely to go?' Rose hugged to herself the certainty that destiny was at last on her side and that her life and Joe's were now irrevocably entwined.

Which was why she broke a lifetime's habit and took herself off on a shopping spree. Alas, when at last she needed them, those expert shoppers, Bunty and Lily, were no longer around to guide her and show her the ropes. Harrods seemed the best place to start, with so much beneath one roof. She had only been there a couple of times as a very disgruntled child. She found it vast and completely changed; they seemed to have swapped the departments round but her ruthless drive and determination aided her in her quest.

Of all the clothes she had ever had, due to Bunty's taste and flair the dress she had worn to the Oxford ball had produced the most flattering comments. Although she rarely exercised, she was naturally slim and still a size eight. She carefully cruised the designer rails, searching for something understated and chic that would have the desired effect on Joe and perhaps lead him to propose. She was horrified by some of the price tags but earned a lot which she rarely spent. And nothing was more important now than making the right impression.

At last she found at St Laurent a smart two-piece in the requisite shade. 'It goes with your eyes,' the salesgirl said, which must be all to the good. 'Is it for a special occasion?' she asked as she carefully wrapped it in tissue.

Rose hesitated then blushed. 'For my wedding,' she said.

The girl was thrilled. 'And when is that?'

'In a couple of months,' Rose said.

'Wait,' said the girl and hurried away, returning with a matching bag. 'From St Laurent with our compliments,' she said.

People were nice. Rose smiled and moved on, as exhilarated as if it were true. On an impulse she stopped at Lancôme for a makeover.

'Madam has wonderful eyes,' said the girl, skilfully blending the colours together. '*April in Paris*, I think, works best to bring out that glorious green.'

Forty minutes and two hundred pounds later, Rose emerged, feeling like a star, then spent twice as much on a pair of Jimmy Choo shoes. On the taxi ride home (she was too tired to walk and somehow the bus didn't fit the occasion) she closed her eyes in euphoria and allowed herself to drift off.

'You look happy,' the driver said as she tipped him a generous twenty per cent. 'Off on your holidays, are you?' he asked.

'My honeymoon,' said Rose.

41

Sometimes on Sundays Joe and Rose would drive out to Twickenham for lunch with Bunty and Matthew. They took the baby in a carrycot and placed her carefully on the couch alongside her deeply grieving grandmother, still shattered by what had occurred. Bunty had aged almost overnight. Instead of the radiant Chelsea blonde who had passed herself off as an older sister, she suddenly looked her age which was getting on for sixty. The veins stood out on her bird-like hands and the nails were no longer immaculately groomed. Her hair had thinned; her scalp was showing through.

Rose would efficiently bottle-feed Daisy then burp her like a practised nurse. Joe and Matthew looked on in silence, united in a mixture of sadness and pride. It was too soon to know who Daisy took after but she did have distinctive aspects of Rose. When the milk was finished she would scream and kick and flail her tiny fists, demanding more.

'Come to me, precious.' Bunty roused herself and gathered the baby on to her lap. 'She's the image of Lily at this age.' Which set her off crying again.

Rose rescued Daisy and held her tight. Feelings she'd never experienced before made her all soft inside. She had never been so overwhelmed by anything living. But this was Joe's daughter, flesh of his flesh. She nuzzled her nose in the small creature's neck, then looked up to find the father's eyes upon her. In them she detected a new emotion that, in her newly hyper state, she wrongly translated as love.

Matthew, watching, was indescribably touched. Something intrinsic had changed in Rose. His hard-headed bluestocking daughter at last was showing a more human side.

These days she'd started to look much better with her sleek bobbed hair and eyes made up to accentuate their colour. Her clothes had improved; he had noticed that too the first time he'd seen her alone with Joe. Bunty had been right all along. If Lily's dying had achieved anything, it was this.

Rose carefully handed the baby to Joe and went to the kitchen to check on the lunch. Bunty made an effort to rise but was still uncertain on her feet.

'It's all right, Mum, I can manage,' said Rose. 'Stay

where you are and bond with your grandchild.'
Another apparent miracle. Suddenly she could cook.

The cookery course had been pure inspiration. She
had picked up a leaflet in a hardware store and, on a
whim, signed up for ten basic lessons. She was sick
of her own shabby repertoire, beans from the can or
a takeaway. When she came home late, her energy
drained, she was used to eating alone. She never bothered to set the table, ate from the pan as she flicked
through her mail. But her life had now taken on new
dimensions. The Fates had finally come to their senses
and delivered up Daisy and Joe.

Only Esther knew of the course, handily close in
Elizabeth Street, and even she thought hard before
making a comment. Rose was suddenly looking
smarter, had acquired the knack of subtle makeup,
was even streaking her hair. She was thirty-five, not
yet in her prime, and doing exceedingly well in her
job. On the grapevine Esther heard only good things
about her. So why the cooking? It was hard to tell.
She certainly seemed now a lot more content. As well
as besotted with Lily's baby which made her a much
nicer person.

Meg, now increasingly wary of Rose, laughed cynically at the notion.

'Rose in an apron? That I'd love to see though I

would be wary of sampling her cooking. There's some-thing very Lucrezia Borgia about her.'

Which summed it up. Meg was not a fool. Esther couldn't believe she'd been taken in. Again Rose had an ulterior motive. How could she have thought she might have changed?

So here was Rose now, in her mother's kitchen, basting the roast like a seasoned pro, draining the juices and keeping some back for the gravy. Joe could carve; he had offered already. Matthew was also showing signs of great strain. Both the Prescotts were greatly dimin-ished since losing a second child. On cue, Joe came in, getting ice for the drinks, and asked if she fancied a pre-lunch cocktail. No, said Rose. She needed her wits about her. How totally different they were, the sisters. He remembered how effortless cooking had been for his wife.

'Do you need any help?'

'No, thank you,' she said. 'I just have to do the potatoes.' Her smile was unprecedentedly sweet. Though still not remotely in Lily's league, she was making the best of herself these days perhaps because, at last, she was suddenly needed. Joe didn't complain; without her he'd never have coped.

'Is Daisy all right?'

'Asleep,' he said. Curled up on the lap of his mother-in-law. While Matthew, in the familiar way, was deep in the Sunday papers.

Joe lingered on and watched Rose at work. He had always admired her impressive brain. The tension that once had existed between them was mellowing into true friendship.

'Do you want me to carry anything in?'

Rose was startled. 'No thank you,' she said. Joe and domestic ordinariness didn't mix. She needed him still on his pedestal, the man she had worshipped for so many years. Since the birth of Daisy and Lily's death he was treating her like a real person.

'If you need me, just holler.' He picked up the ice and went back into the drawing room to preside.

He felt at home now in this house though the image of Lily was fading fast. What they'd had together had been tenuous and could not have survived. He had a major decision to make that might have bearing on all their lives. The Prescott family had propped him up and helped him through his darkest hour. Now, however, it was time to move on. He could not delay it for very much longer. He had done what he could to pay his dues. A whole different future lay ahead.

42

The nursery maid would have to go. Rose didn't much care for her attitude. Added to which she was too young, eighteen, the dangerous age. Joe now, of course, was more mature, had steadied a lot since his daughter's birth, but Rose wasn't risking anything; she needed to be in control. Carmel was Spanish with come hither eyes and an irritatingly silly laugh. Daisy was growing attached to her, another good reason she should go. The child was at the age when she'd most miss her mother and must not be permitted to bond with anyone but her aunt. Rose spied on Carmel till she found an excuse to fire her on the spot with two weeks' wages.

Joe was surprised. He had liked the girl but had weightier things on his mind right now. He was glad he had Rose to help sort out his household. Through an ad in *The Lady* she found Therese, a professional nanny of forty-two. This one, though, need not live in. She rented a room in a hostel round the corner. Rose started reading childcare books for when they would not need a nanny at all. She hinted to Joe that she might move in; there was room enough for all three of them. She could easily let her flat if he'd just say the word.

Joe, though, had other things on his mind, was back to keeping late hours again. Rose got to the flat before Therese left then stuck around, with a meal prepared, until he at last showed up.

'Thanks,' he said, back to being withdrawn. 'You shouldn't have waited. I could have coped. You do have a life of your own.'

'No problem,' said Rose. 'I love spending time with Daisy.'

Although Joe appeared not to want her around, Rose blindly refused to acknowledge the hint. Even a hard-working man like him must loosen up at times. She would stay and share the meal with him and ask him questions about his day, ignoring the fact that, increasingly, he appeared preoccupied. She grew impatient, expecting more; felt she got less respect than was her due. After all, without her intervention, even though he still didn't know it, he wouldn't be here at all.

After they'd eaten, she cleared away while Joe

withdrew to his study to work. He treated her like a housekeeper now. Her patience was wearing thin.

The dream persisted nonetheless. It could only be a matter of time. She had to make Joe see where his true happiness lay. She started producing opera tickets, claiming that she had been stood up. It worked a couple of times then Joe backed off.

'Look,' he said with a tentative smile. 'You know I'm grateful for all you do. You mean a great deal to Daisy and me but you mustn't neglect your own life.' She was spending more time down in Twickenham too, propping up her parents. Matthew seemed not to be at all well and Bunty was visibly fading. Lily's death had taken its toll. It was like a light going out.

Rose was appalled. This was not what she'd planned. Her life was devoted to all of them. With Lily gone, they needed her more, something she'd always wanted.

'Nonsense,' she said. 'We are family now. Lily would want us to be together.' They never mentioned the murder or if Lily had done it.

'She was always temperamental,' said Rose on a rare occasion when somebody asked a highly impertinent question. 'The problem was, they spoilt her to death. The nine years between us meant she grew up, more or less, as an only child, allowed to run amok.'

'But she had the sweetest disposition.' It was still an unthinkable tragedy. How well Joe recalled the child she had been the first time their paths had crossed.

'Thwarted in love. That was what she was.' Rose spoke with a hint of satisfaction. 'When that predatory woman came on the scene, Lily lost her rag.'

Joe, who knew the truth, closed his eyes. The guilt he felt was unbearable. There'd been nothing between him and Sukey Khan though he knew that no one believed that. The girl was pretty and he was her boss. Say no more: the equation added up. But fancy Lily with that lethal hatpin. It still sent shivers down everyone's spine. Despite Joe's caustic withdrawn persona, it was thrilling to think what passions he'd roused. Women looked at him in a different way. Rose was all too aware of that. If he hadn't done the deed himself, he was certainly party to it. At least, Ann Cole and her much reduced set were still propagating that theory. He might have sued for slander but couldn't care less.

It was Esther who broke the news to Rose who was only grateful that Ann didn't get in first. Joe had been summoned to see the PM and asked to stay on for a further three years. His work had been exemplary; the Cabinet was anxious not to lose him. Joe said he'd certainly give it some thought though still felt a duty to MIT. Circumstances, of course, had changed things a lot.

'Take your time,' the Prime Minister said and suggested he took a three-month break during which he could return to the States to decide where his loyalties lay.

'This time,' said Esther, 'he'll get that knighthood.' A shame, she thought though did not say aloud, that even in this poor Lily had lost. She'd have loved to have been a Lady.

Rose, who had not seen it coming, was appalled. There was nothing left in the States for Joe. She was his family now and Daisy, plus the ailing Twickenham folk. He must not think of breaking those ties. At the very least, he owed it to the child.

She was waiting when he came home that night, wearing the outfit she'd bought with a wedding in mind.

'Rose. How nice.' He barely glanced at her but hung his overcoat in the closet as if playing for time.

She poured him a drink like a dutiful wife then perched herself at the end of the couch, showing off her figure, she felt, to its best advantage. It was now or never; she hadn't much time. If he got away, as she felt was possible, she couldn't imagine what might happen next. She lit them each a cigarette, swung back her hair and confronted him, green eyes narrowed and blazing with accusation.

'You are going back to the States,' she said. 'Did you never think of consulting me? We are your family now, myself and Daisy.'

'It isn't official yet,' he said. 'It's confidential until I decide.' He frowned. He was clearly not pleased that she had found out.

'And what about Daisy while you're gone?' Foolish hope was renewing itself as her agile brain concocted an alternative plan. She would do as she'd always wanted to, move in here for the interim. It would give her time alone with the child in which to cement their relationship. Daisy would grieve while Rose would become the mother she'd never known.

For a long thoughtful moment Joe stared at her, exhaling smoke without saying a word. Tonight his eyes were basilisk hard; he was a man well used to authority, all trace of sentimentality now quite gone. A man who had spurned her several times. By now she should really have known what to expect.

'She's coming with me of course,' he said. 'What did you think? She's my daughter.'

43

He closed up the flat and dismissed the nanny. His future, he told her, was undecided so he could not expect her to hang around until he had definite plans. If he wanted her back he would let her know in good time. He tipped her well. Rose wasn't allowed to see them off because it would be too disruptive for Daisy. The airline would help him take care of her on the flight. Nevertheless, she kept her keys in case an emergency should arise. She would look in now and again, she said, and keep an eye on things. There was no real need, there was porter service, but Joe knew enough not to argue with her. He sensed how bitterly hurt she was but his daughter, along with his own career, came first.

Parting from Bunty was far more painful. He was taking away the one thing she had left to love. Or so it seemed now; he was gentle with her. Drove out there with Daisy to say goodbye and promised to keep them both up to date with her progress. Matthew, he thought, was not looking well; he was puffy-faced and had a corpse-like pallor. Any exertion caused him to wheeze. Something was obviously wrong.

'Do take care of yourselves,' said Joe. 'Daisy needs you and so do I. Have you ever thought of asking Rose to move in?' Apart from anything she could do for them, it might take her mind off him.

Matthew winced. 'She is too much trouble.'

The two of them swapped a reciprocal grin. Still, she had been helpful since Lily died.

'I hope by the time we see you again,' said Joe, 'you will both be back in fighting form.'

Joe's leaving was like a slap in the face. Rose couldn't believe he could just opt out. Her engagement plans would now have to be put on hold.

'You will be back?'

'I'll let you know.' But don't wait up, he wanted to say. It all came back, those terrible Oxford confrontations.

She wept as she watched them drive away. She'd have been at the airport if Joe hadn't asked her not to. But she still had his flat to oversee so dropped in there whenever she could. To check that everything was all right, she regularly told the porter. A flashback of Sukey doing the same occasionally caused her heart to chill. Every time, she went through Joe's things, though looking for what she didn't know. Some sign, she supposed, of a secret life despite the fact that he didn't appear to have one.

Lily's things were still there, untouched. If Bunty had been in better shape, they'd have had them sorted by now and off to Oxfam. Instead Rose was left to manage alone, something she'd grown accustomed to. The family closeness had ended with Lily's death. She tried on the clothes, which were slightly too tight. Lily was slimmer though more curvaceous. She picked her way through the jewellery box, impressed by some of the pieces her sister possessed. Joe had been very generous, especially at the start when he'd been besotted with her.

The things that looked the most valuable Rose wrapped in a scarf and took home with her. They'd be safer there where no passing thief was ever likely to look. The engagement ring she kept for herself; their hands had been similar, small and well formed. She'd remember to put it back before Joe's return.

The flat had a state of the art TV as well as a de luxe hi-fi system and Joe's eclectic collection of classic CDs. Rose, who felt stultified at home, got into the habit of eating there as she had in the days leading up to

Jean-Paul's death. She wondered now how Annette was faring, had not heard a word from her recently. Not even, which was odder, when Lily died. She thought about that; it was not like Annette. There was no way she couldn't have heard the news, especially since the coverage had centred so closely on Joe. It might be a question of delicacy. Annette was sensitive and refined. Having recently been bereaved herself, she would certainly empathise.

Rose decided to write to her. She felt they'd developed a strong connection and now that Joe was back in the States she could use her as a spy. Annette knew of her feelings for Joe, had sympathised and offered support. Had urged her not to give up hope though that was, of course, pre-Lily. She could think of nobody she had liked more, envied the closeness the Gerards had shared. Through knowing each other from Junior High they had been fundamentally in tune. Not just lovers but friends as well, which was where she and Joe had started off. With the growth of her fantasy, Rose lost control of the truth.

It seemed to her now, alone in Joe's flat, a glass of his bourbon in her hand, that things might have turned out differently had Lily not intervened. If, on the night of the opera, Joe had met her in town and not come to the house, she was certain they would be together now. And had he not been there nine years before and caught the child fooling about by the tree, the disastrous marriage would never have taken place. Lily had always been a flirt. Even at nine she was poison.

Rose took to wearing Lily's ring though not to the office: she was smarter than that. But out of hours she would slip it on and even had manicures to enhance it. The manicurist was most impressed: the diamonds were costly and perfectly matched. She asked when the wedding was going to be. Rose told her, as soon as her partner returned from abroad. She resurrected the wedding collage she had hidden since Lily and Joe had come home and put it back on the table next to her bed. She kissed it before she went to sleep and placed Lily's ring beside it.

Out of the blue, she heard from Hugo who sent a belated condolence note. He'd have been in touch before, he explained, but had only just heard the news. He was speechless with sadness, found it hard to believe. Lily had been such a lovely kid. He had been in Athens researching a book but now was home and would love to see Rose, if only for old times' sake.

'I'll give you a call,' he scrawled at the end. 'It has been too long. I miss you.'

Rose considered then made up her mind. There was no point raking over might-have-beens. She acknowledged that Hugo had been a good friend but now was not the time for raising his hopes. She thanked him for his condolences which she would, she promised, pass on to her parents. She wasn't able to see him, though, because she was soon to be married.

44

Annette's reply to her friendly letter was disappointingly lacking in news. Yes, she had known about Lily, she said; had been in continuous touch with Joe. He was very brave she was glad to report, and despite the tragic circumstances seemed to be bearing up surprisingly well. The baby, of course, was an absolute joy as well as a much needed solace for him. She herself was learning to cope. Life without Jean-Paul was very lonely. No, she had no current plans for coming over. She didn't ask about Rose at all but did, politely, wish her well.

Rose continued to haunt Joe's flat, retreating further into make-believe as she reconstructed a past that had never existed. The single abortive night they had shared transformed itself now into mega romance. She ran the heavily edited tape endlessly through her warped mind. He had loved her once and would do so again.

She sent him a string of chirpy notes as well as small gifts for Daisy.

Esther knew nothing about Joe's plans except that he'd taken sabbatical leave in order to sort out his future and his daughter's. His contribution to public life was so important in Parliament that every concession was being made to enable him to return when he was ready. He had been through a truly horrendous time. Public sympathy turned again to him.

'It was smart of him to go,' she said, unknowingly echoing Ann's same thought. The case had attracted huge interest so that, even though his name had been cleared, it was better to absent himself until the collective memory had faded. The nature of the killing was such that public consensus recoiled in disgust. The use of a hatpin had been especially nasty.

Rose was impervious to this view. The choice of weapon was incidental, had served to get rid of that parasite, Sukey, in a fast and effective way. Murder was no big deal if it served a purpose.

'You are surely over him now,' Esther said, surprised when Rose leapt to Joe's defence. She was fully in tune with Ann Cole's decree that there's rarely smoke without fire. She was sorry that Hugo had defected. He had struck her as a decent bloke as well as a steadying influence on Rose.

'I can't understand why you let him go.' He had

always been such a rock of devotion whose constancy had surely deserved better treatment.

'He bored me,' said Rose, which was simply not true. She didn't want Esther to know what she had done.

And all for what? Even she now had doubts. Joe was no more in touch than before. She kept him informed of every detail connected in any way with his flat even though there was a management team to deal with matters like service charges and rent. She made it her business to talk to them and check on even the slightest thing, all of which she relayed to Joe. He rarely bothered to answer.

She was also thinking of Daisy's future by checking out local nursery schools. She'd no longer need a nanny when they returned. She kept the child's photograph on her desk and told people proudly it was her niece. The poor little soul had lost her mother; she might consider adopting her in order to help bring her up.

'Doesn't she have a father?' they'd ask.

Rose smiled and feigned sudden bashfulness. 'She does,' she said. 'We plan to raise her together.'

Tongues were wagging; the rumours increased. This was the child of the killer, they knew, who had murdered one of their own in a very sick way. How brave and self-effacing Rose was. They might not like her but all agreed she had guts.

*   *   *

Weekends were mainly now spent with her parents, attempting to rouse them from apathy and help get their lives back on course; they had lost their way. Bunty had now become very confused. Her short-term memory was impaired and she sometimes even looked vague when Rose turned up. At her most alarming, she called her Lily and fretted to know where the baby had gone. Rose quickly tired of putting her right so left her with the illusion.

Matthew's behaviour had not changed much though now he rarely got out of his chair and, worryingly, left the crossword puzzle unfinished.

'They are slowly atrophying,' said Rose, meeting Esther for a rare supper. 'Yet they're not that old. Both still in their prime. A year ago my mother was making hats.'

'It's the shock.' Esther had no medical knowledge but had heard of this situation before. When faced with such a catastrophe, people lost the will to live.

'They still have me.' Again she was bitter. Esther, understanding, gave her a hug.

'They have, indeed. And in time they may rally.' Matthew, maybe, though not Bunty from what she had heard.

Rose seemed to be coping remarkably well, doing the laundry and cooking them meals. She filled the freezer with ready-made dishes to heat up during the week.

'I'll say this for her,' Esther said to Meg. 'She's improved a lot in the past few months.' Where once her sister had dominated, Rose had come into her own.

'What about the boyfriend?' asked Meg, sick of the ongoing saga of Rose. The few times they'd met, she had found her cool and dismissive.

'He never really existed,' said Esther. 'Not in the way she would have you believe. All they ever were was a one night stand, and even then he was drunk.'

It was pitiful really, she had to admit, when faced with the harsh reality. Her childhood friend with the brilliant mind was, like her mother, now showing signs of delusion. She talked to strangers she met on the bus, showing them photographs of her child. Not yet a year, she said, and already talking.

'Really?' they'd say as they edged away. The fanatical light in her eye was distinctly disturbing.

And still she did not hear from him. The gifts and letters went unacknowledged. She started sending them registered which failed to elicit a response. So, instead, she turned to her principal ally, Annette.

'Is Joe all right?' The call came late, just as Annette was nodding off. She groped for the light in alarm till she knew who it was.

'Rose,' she said. 'You quite startled me. In Massachusetts it's after ten. Where you are it must be the middle of the night. Couldn't it wait till morning?'

She had picked up the fact that Rose's voice was slurred. She must have been hitting the bottle again. She wondered if she was in Joe's flat. She knew he didn't like that.

'Is he all right? I need to know.' The voice had reached its familiar whine. 'He neither answers my letters nor takes my calls.'

'He's fine,' said Annette, at her soothing best, familiar now with these late night calls. 'I think you should get some sleep and talk in the morning.'

'Nor does he call of his own accord.'

'He is very busy,' was all she could say. 'Making plans for his future life. He has a lot on his mind.' She knew she was taking a chance but so what. Placating Rose was a massive bore. It wasn't even as if they had ever been friends.

'How do you know that?'

'We speak,' she said.

'He never talks to me any more.'

'Good night.'

45

In the office, though, Rose continued effective, subduing subversion with glacial force. She had reached the pinnacle of her power; few ever dared confront her. Of course they whispered behind her back about the murder that had rocked them all. The ghastly death of an enigmatic colleague whom not all had liked but who had still not deserved to die so horrifically. It was as well that the sister died too, though how Rose could carry on as normal was beyond their comprehension. But, since she encouraged no intimacy, none was in a position to suss that out.

The word was that she and her brother-in-law had been closer than they should have been. Certainly it was his child whose picture she displayed on her desk. Now he was gone, for a while at least, back to the fastness of MIT. Whether or not he'd return was not yet known. Rose ignored all gossip, remained aloof, continued to work like an automaton. No matter how much they threw at her, she got through it with lightning speed.

She started picking on subordinates, became increasingly hard to please. Research she had requested went back annotated in red like schoolwork. Could do better, she virtually scrawled. The department was not amused.

'Who does she think she is?' they asked, she with her high and mighty ways. She no longer acknowledged them in the street or sat with them in the works canteen. She ate at her desk and got on with things, oblivious of what was going on around her.

Professionally, though, she was highly respected, could still perform feats that others could not. The speed of her calculating brain continued to dazzle her peers.

'She is like a human computer,' they said. And all with no effort at all.

At night, when she wasn't invading Joe's space, she hunched at home over calculations, listening to music as she worked. Bach and Handel helped to calm her, keeping her wilder illusions at bay. The harder the problem she set herself, the saner she remained. She would work till ten, then take a break, which was when the craziness would emerge. A couple of whiskies and she was off, spiralling out of control.

These were the times she wrote to Joe, the words so jumbled they spilled off the page, no longer coherent, a demented mishmash of longing. She accused him, implored him, adored him, the lot, swinging from sadness to wild euphoria, reminding him of times they had shared, many of them made up. Repeatedly she returned to the night she had first encountered him in Rick's Bar, a cigarette stuck to his lower lip, his eyes half closed as he played. She recalled the time they had first made love, ignoring the fact it was also the last and that she had no recollection of the act. She told him he had broken her heart but that she had now forgiven him. She'd be waiting for him when he returned; was still taking care of his flat.

In the morning she often destroyed the letters or put them away in a drawer. Now and again, however, she'd send them off. It made no difference: he never replied, had cut her out of his life it seemed. When, despairing, she called Annette her message service was on. She crossed off the days Joe would be away and the closer it got to the end of the three months, the wilder she became.

Esther met Hugo in the street, hailing him with unfeigned joy.

'Hi!' she said. 'How are you, stranger? Where have you been hiding all this time?'

'Working,' he said. He liked her too. He told her a bit about his job. His hair was shorter, he seemed less of a wimp; could now look her straight in the eye. He had, it appeared, grown up. It suited him.

Esther, too, had improved a lot and looked what she was, a rising politician. She said she would like to stay in touch. Perhaps he'd come over one night for a meal. She gave him her card and said not to leave it too long.

Just as she was turning away, he stopped her with a sudden thought. 'Rose,' he inquired. 'Is she married yet?' He'd received no notification.

'Married?' said Esther, mildly shocked, having no idea where he'd got that from.

'That was the reason she gave,' he explained, 'for not seeing me any more.'

Esther reeled. Now Rose had gone too far. 'You must have misunderstood,' she said. 'She is still very much on the loose. Why not give her a ring?'

'No,' said Hugo and shook his head. There had been no mistake; he had it in writing. He walked away with a sad expression. If she'd wanted to end the relationship, at least she need not have lied.

'She always was a bitch,' said Meg when Esther regaled her with what Rose had done. 'I never liked her. You're far too soft. Just because you knew each other at school.'

'She used to be my best friend,' said Esther. Though, sadly, not any longer.

'How could you treat him like that?' Esther asked the next time she met up with Rose. 'You didn't have to tell such a blatant lie.'

Rose merely shrugged. She didn't care. 'What difference does it make?' she asked. 'He hung around like a puppy dog, was getting on my nerves.'

'Hugo was a good friend to you and deserved better treatment,' Esther said. 'In any case, why that particular lie? You knew he was bound to find out.'

Again she shrugged. 'It was not a lie,' she said as she lit a cigarette. 'I *am* getting married. Just haven't yet set a date.'

Esther stared. This was worse than she'd feared. Her friend was clearly now barking mad.

'And who is the lucky man?' she asked.

Rose looked astonished. 'You know.'

Neither spoke for a minute or two then Esther leaned over and took Rose's hand. 'Don't you think,' she said, 'we should talk about it?'

Rose looked defiant. 'There's nothing to say. You have always known how I feel about Joe. We were, from the start, intended for each other. Lily was nothing but an aberration.'

'But he's gone,' said Esther. 'And won't be back. I

heard it myself from Downing Street. He is signing again with MIT. They are really sorry to lose him.'

'When was that?' Rose was deathly pale. The hand with the cigarette started to shake. 'It can't be true. He hasn't told me. And I am the person closest to him. His best friend.'

'What did you say?' Meg asked Esther later.

'Just that I must have been misinformed. I hadn't the heart to do otherwise or else she'd have really lost it.'

46

Matthew called to say Bunty had fallen. He didn't want to leave her, he said.

'Then call Social Services,' snapped Rose. 'And don't ring me during the day.'

She was growing frenzied. There was still no word so she'd started ringing Annette again. Night or day made no difference. She had to find out what was going on. At MIT no one answered Joe's line. He was on a sabbatical she was told when, in frustration, she worked her way through to the switchboard.

'He *is* there,' she said. 'I've been writing to him.'

'And did he ever reply?' was the courteous response.

'Yes.' Well, no. What they said was true. The sole connection she'd had was via Annette.

'We have no formal instructions on that.' The operator, before ringing off, advised her to take it higher.

Meanwhile Matthew was in a sweat. He had

managed to get Bunty back on her feet and then to the couch in the living room, where she collapsed. She seemed confused. When would Lily be home? Matthew calmed her and made her tea. He would drive her to the doctor himself if it weren't for the pain in his chest.

'Come on, old girl. You will be all right.' He wrapped a travelling rug round her legs. If only Rose weren't so far away. And so consistently busy.

Annette lay low. She had nothing to say and was sick of fielding Rose's calls. Rose seemed to consider her a friend when, in fact, they were only acquaintances who'd met just a couple of times. Lily she'd known and liked far more. She'd been younger, fresher and truly naïve. She didn't feel good about what she was going to do.

'Tell her yourself.'

'I can't,' said Joe. He could well imagine how she'd react; come over and make a colossal fuss. He couldn't take any more. Whenever he thought he'd got rid of her, she returned a hundred times more clingy. Left to himself, he'd do nothing at all. She was bound to find out soon enough. And if she never did, it was all to the good.

'Well, you must tell the Prescotts. It is only fair. Before they hear from some other source.'

Reluctantly he agreed she was right. They were, after all, Daisy's grandparents who would always be part of her life.

'Call them today.'

'I would rather write.' News of this kind was never easy; he wanted to give them space to take it in. Both were in a sharp decline; a shock might drive them over the edge. But that was nothing to what it would do to Rose which was why he prevaricated.

'Well, please don't leave it too long,' begged Annette with a sigh.

They'd not heard from Joe in quite a while. Bunty fretted about the baby. 'He must be due back soon,' she said, though could no longer recall what they had been told.

Matthew grunted. He thought so too but hesitated to raise her hopes. Joe, these days, was a man of distinction, courted by governments worldwide for his specialist expertise. Fancy their Lily marrying him, though, as it turned out, she'd have been better served had they never met. It was Rose's fault.

Matthew was hardly working these days, had left the practice to his younger partners. Whenever he hauled himself into town, he came home utterly shattered. Another result of Lily's death. He feared neither of them would ever recover. He was saddened by

Bunty's deterioration. She was no longer the girl he had married; had lost her sparkling radiance the day her daughter died. So it was vital that they see Daisy as soon as it could be arranged.

'I'll talk to Rose.' If she'd take his call. He hesitated to interrupt her at work in case she bit his head off.

He finally reached her that night at home. She sounded not a little distrait.

'Yes?' she said with a hopeful note that went when she recognised his voice. 'Dad,' she asked him testily. 'What now?'

No one spoke to Matthew that way, least of all his daughter. Despite his flagging energy and the constant nagging ache in his chest, his dignity returned. He swiftly pulled rank.

'You mother is not at all well,' he said. 'It wouldn't hurt if you came to see her. She is fretting still. You would know that if you ever bothered to check.'

'I can't talk now. I'm expecting a call.' Rose didn't sound at all like herself. If he didn't know her better, he'd say she'd been drinking.

'Have you heard from Joe when he's coming back? That's all it is, she is missing the child.' Pride and irritation stopped him spelling out the truth.

'Soon,' said Rose vaguely. 'I'll let you know. It should have been several weeks ago. I heard that from Ten

Downing Street. He must have been delayed.' She was definitely sloshed; her voice was slurred.

He disapproved but did not comment. It wasn't his business any more. For goodness' sake, she was middle-aged, getting on for forty.

'Speak to your mother some time,' he said. 'Better still, come and visit us. I know you have a taxing job but get your priorities right.'

Rose said nothing so Matthew rang off. Sometimes he couldn't believe what a monster he'd raised.

In the end they took the coward's way out. They would not be around when Rose heard the news. Joe wrote to say he was not coming back. He was staying on at MIT and, by the way, marrying Annette. In some ways it seemed inevitable. He had always loved her, right from the start, as soulmate, confidante and friend, not just as Jean-Paul's wife. Secret guilt at his growing feelings had prompted him to accept the job in London in an attempt to put space between them. Time had passed and now things had changed. The terrible early loss of Jean-Paul had freed them to be together without dishonour. They'd done nothing wrong. They both owed a debt to Rose for acting cupid.

They would never stop being family, he said, and Daisy would come and visit when she was older. He would always be indebted to Rose for all she had done after Lily died. For looking after the flat and propping him up. He would tell her parents himself, he said. He knew how much they were missing Daisy. When their health was improved they must come and stay; there was plenty of room in the house.

47

Rose's scream could be heard three floors up. She was getting ready for work but called in sick. She read the letter several times, unable to come to terms with the news. Her initial instinct was total denial, a tasteless joke they had conjured up that was disrespectful to Lily and Jean-Paul. She got as far as dialling the States then reconsidered and hung up. It was morning; she was totally sober. She knew enough not to act on impulse. This devastating shock had thrown her off course. It didn't stop her, though, ringing Esther, ignoring the fact that she was at work, to say it was imperative that they meet.

Esther's sigh was deeply felt. She had feared that something like this might occur. What had started off as a childish crush had veered into lunacy. There was nothing now she could do but repeat what she had endlessly said before. Watch my lips: he doesn't love you and, furthermore, never did. Meg would say, in her caustic way, it was long overdue that Rose grew up. Faced with her, though, with her shell-shocked glaze, Esther could not be that cruel. Instead she held her tight in her arms until the sobbing abated.

'When do you think it began?' she asked, similarly shaken by the news. It was less than a year since Lily's death. How could he marry again so soon? She had known, of course, he would not return. Now she blamed herself for not having said so more forcefully.

Miserably Rose just shook her head. It was all a mystery to her. The Gerards had been Joe's closest friends. Which was, more or less, all she really knew about them. She had liked Annette, with her throaty chuckle and the warmth and sincerity in her eyes. Now it appeared her assessment had been wrong.

'She pretended to be my friend,' she sobbed. 'They bought me dinner at the Savoy.' She quite forgot what Esther knew, that that had been one of the only two times they had met.

'She wasn't your friend, she was Lily's,' said Esther but Rose was unwilling to listen to sense.

'She snatched him from under my nose. I will never forgive her.'

So now Annette would get to raise Daisy. She had always wanted a child of her own. To practical Esther, who was firmly earthed, the situation made excellent sense. And, as for the speed of the whole thing, both had recently been bereaved. They had probably clung to each other in their grief. And why not?

Needless to say, Rose was not convinced, was muttering now about faithlessness. 'I wonder how long they'd been carrying on.' Her face twisted into a spasm of hate as she spat out the venomous words.

'Don't go jumping to false conclusions.' The last thing Rose needed was a vendetta. Joe wasn't, and never had been, hers. Perhaps, at last, she would learn to face that fact.

'I'm going out there to confront her,' said Rose. 'She must understand he belongs to me.' The thought of Annette with her sister's child made her want to destroy things and throw up.

Esther did all she could to calm her though her words were simply not sinking in. The Sukey rumours had been bad enough. And look what had happened there.

'At least think it through before you go. And please consider your parents, too. At a time like this they need you here and not fighting duels in the States.'

Matthew and Bunty were disappointed but put their granddaughter's well-being first. Lily had been very close to Annette who was, from all accounts, a very good friend. She was older than Lily, almost Joe's age, herself a scientist of repute. She had never had children of her own, due to her husband's slowly diminishing health.

'She gave up a lot for him,' Bunty said, remembering now all she'd heard from Lily. Annette had known a while before Jean-Paul died that his future was very uncertain. Joe, of course, remained a wild card who needed a woman of character to control him.

'Good luck to them both,' said Matthew firmly, concealing his own inner pain.

'Will we get to see Daisy again?' Bunty was fearful of losing touch.

'Of course,' said Matthew. 'He says so in the letter.'

Secretly he was less convinced but resolved he would never let Bunty know. A brand new marriage so far away would not do a lot for continuing ties. If Bunty's health declined any more, he could not be assured of a happy outcome. 'Perhaps they will have more children,' he said. 'And make you an honorary granny.'

Bunty smiled weakly though didn't applaud. In her more lucid moments she had an idea of what was happening to her. But Matthew came first, as he always had. She struggled gamely from her chair and went to prepare his tea.

* * *

Rose remained still incandescent. Her fury grew with each passing breath. Her colleagues hid when they saw her coming for fear of a confrontation. News of Joe's marriage was swiftly out and the gossip machines were soon cranking up. Foremost in the attack was Ann Cole whose credibility now seemed restored.

'I always knew there was something going on.' Her sloe-black eyes were sharp with malice. 'This one had better watch her step if she doesn't want to end up in Bluebeard's room.'

Everyone laughed. Ann was a caution who never knew where to draw the line.

'Don't let Rose hear you or you'll be mincemeat,' one said.

They are laughing behind my back, thought Rose, more desolate than she had ever been. They looked on her as a sad old maid, which was true. She lost all incentive to look her best. Her clothes grew shabby, her hair was a mess. On Daisy's birthday she sent a cheque then ground her teeth when a letter arrived from Annette. Daisy was growing fast, she said, and would soon be going to nursery school. Annette had given up work for a year, in order to bond with her.

'We are planting a garden in Lily's memory,' she wrote, 'which I hope will be Daisy's special place. We are buying a rose bush with your cheque so that every time it blooms, she'll think of you.'

It was, Esther said, a generous thought which showed how selfless Annette must be. Rose said nothing but shook with a rage that threatened to consume her.

48

Overnight Rose appeared to age, having lost the spring in her step. The clatter of her heels went too; she switched to wearing old lady shoes. She also abandoned her contact lenses. They were too much trouble and all of a sudden she no longer cared how she looked. She developed a barely perceptible stoop, hinting at early osteoporosis. All the fight had drained from her except when it came to office feuds. Her tongue grew sharper as her humour waned. She made a tenacious foe. At work they tried to steer clear of her. Confrontation, however minor, could erupt into sudden war. Cross Rose and you might as well clear your desk and move to another department.

Communication with Joe and Annette accordingly shrank to a trickle. Rose would have nothing to do with them so the onus descended on Matthew. It wasn't easy for him these days having to prop up Bunty alone with his energy gone and his own health on the decline. But he didn't complain. That little girl in America became the focus of their lives. They never saw her but wrote to her as often as they were able.

'One day, when she is old enough, she will write and tell us about herself.' From the snaps Annette sent she showed a resemblance to Rose.

Bunty grew vaguer and was seldom at ease, unable to grasp the most ordinary facts. If left on her own for more than short breaks, she would have an anxiety attack.

'Please come and see her. She needs you,' Matthew said. These days his calls to Rose verged on the pleading. The least she could do was help prop Bunty up.

'When is Lily coming home?' had become an almost obsessive cry. Matthew concocted elaborate lies to stop Bunty getting upset.

'Rose will be here for Sunday lunch.' He had bribed her by offering to run her back. She didn't like driving in heavy traffic so rarely used her car.

When she did come down she was surly and terse and snapped at her mother for asking the same question twice. 'I told you that five minutes ago. Pay attention. You never seem to listen.'

When Bunty ventured to ask about Hugo, Rose practically bit off her head.

* * *

The fact was she hadn't seen Hugo in months, since that stupid lie about being engaged. She had sneered at him behind his back but now regretted his absence. Esther urged her to drop him a note; he had always had a forgiving nature. But Rose was too stubborn and also too proud to reveal how lonely she was.

'If he wants to see me, he knows where I am.' She closed her mind to the thought of him just as she tried not to think any more about Joe.

Which wasn't easy. He haunted her dreams. She woke in the night with his name on her lips and when she listened to Bach, she often broke down. She focused her hatred upon Annette whom she perceived as a marriage wrecker, ignoring the fact that she'd been a widow long before Lily died. If it weren't for Annette, Joe would still be here and she would be helping him raise his child. The lie she had scribbled to Hugo would, by now, have become the truth.

She patrolled the block on which he had lived even though he had asked her to hand back her keys. She would linger as she passed the door and peer into the lighted hallway. One of the porters knew her by sight and would nod and pass the time of day. She always pretended that she and Joe were still very much an item.

'And the baby?'

'Growing fast,' she would say. 'Toddling now. The image of her mother.'

She bought Daisy toys which she never sent but which gave her the chance to talk about her. As with the trumped-up engagement, she fantasised. Soon the baby turned into her own, her darling Daisy whom she'd left at home.

'She's got a bit of a cough,' she'd explain. 'So I've left her with the nanny.'

With her parents, though, all this bonhomie evaporated. She was only ever grumpy and ungracious when she entered their house.

It was raining hard on this Sunday night and the roads were busy and slicked with water. Rose had something she wanted to do so nagged her father as soon as they left the table.

'Must get back. I've a deadline to meet.' The cold truth was Bunty bored her stiff. From being a sweet, faintly vacuous woman, she had, in her daughter's eyes, lost all her charm. She rattled on about hats in her lucid moments, which were getting rarer, and asked too many times where Lily was.

'For God's sake, can't you shut her up?' Rose had worked herself into a towering rage. She had never been very compassionate even when younger.

'Leave her,' said Matthew. 'She is doing fine. She likes to reminisce about old times.'

It broke his heart to see her like this, the woman

he'd loved now for forty years reduced from a stylish beauty to a vague unstructured wreck. If it weren't for Lily's untimely death he remained convinced she would still be in her prime.

'Have you thought about a home?' asked Rose as she fastened her seat belt and waited for Matthew to close the garage doors before they left.

'Good gracious, no.' He was truly shocked. The way Rose talked about her mother filled him with bitter and helpless fury at what a monster she'd become. Many daughters with no other ties and a house like this within easy reach would have given up the place in town and returned to look after them. He hated the fact that he could no longer properly care for his wife.

'Perhaps you should think about putting her name down. Before she deteriorates any more.' One thing Rose was certain of, she wasn't going to sacrifice herself to cope with either ailing parent.

'Enough!' shouted Matthew. 'I won't have you talking about your mother that way. How can you even think of it? It's outrageous.'

Rose merely shrugged. She was unconcerned. The only person she cared for now was herself.

Matthew fumed as he started the car and edged it into the traffic flow. Why he was bothering to drive her home, he was no longer sure. Rose was a selfish uncaring woman who had never loved anyone in her life apart from that bastard whose playing around had led to the death of his Lily. His flash of rage affected his breathing. He knew he should stop and take a pill but his sole concern right now was to get rid of Rose.

He decided to take a faster route so pulled out into the middle lane but spots were appearing before his eyes; he started to lose control.

'Dad! Watch out!' Rose grabbed the wheel and swung the car out of the path of the lorry. A convenient tree stopped it turning over and rolling into the river.

He was dead before the impact came and wouldn't have known what was going on. Rose, by the purest stroke of luck, emerged from the wreckage unscathed.

49

She got into the habit of waylaying strangers and referring obliquely to her husband, Joe, and the daughter, Daisy, of whom she was so proud. She dressed older than her actual age, wearing long skirts with her sturdy boots and granny specs that went with her greying hair. At work she had her own special fads, organic food which she ate at her desk and making sure that nobody else ever touched her coffee mug. She had no friends; her colleagues steered clear, fearful of her spiteful tongue and the increasingly petty grudges she developed over minor mishaps. She would hammer on about perceived slights and never forgot the most trivial thing while immersing herself in her work, which was still very good. Mathematically speaking, Rose was the best, continually dazzling her cerebral peers. If she weren't so shrewish in her attitudes she'd have been much better liked.

Even Esther saw less of her, pressured by her own burgeoning career but also because of a faintly bad taste in her mouth. Now she thought about it, after all these years, stretching right back to the schooldays they'd shared, she had never known Rose show true emotion apart from her passion for Joe. She had lost a brother and, later, her sister and now her father had tragically died while her mother, too, was very much on the decline. And yet she had seemingly brushed it all off with a startling display of indifference. Had shown no grief nor taken compassionate leave. She had even put up the house for sale, the acme of her father's career for which he'd received architectural awards and page-long obituaries when he died. What meagre love she had ever felt had now transformed into blistering hate; for Annette, supposedly once her friend, and now, inconceivably, even for Joe. Lily had only redeemed herself by dying. She had cast off Hugo with no real excuse and her pride prevented her making amends. He was out there somewhere, should not prove too hard to find.

Even though Meg was opposed to it and couldn't stand Rose, whom she'd never trusted, stalwart Esther refused to give up on her.

'She doesn't give a shit about you. When did you last get a call from her? She's only ever in touch when she's after something.'

Indisputably true. Esther couldn't deny it, knowing Meg only had her best interests at heart. And yet she wouldn't abandon Rose without one final try.

'She can't help the way she is,' she explained. 'Genius like hers has a very dark flipside. She has lived an intensely focused life, deprived of normal emotions.' Slightly mad, she acknowledged that, but ultimately lonely.

Hugo, she knew, would understand. He came from a solidly normal background and had always had a soft spot for Rose despite the way she'd behaved.

'Allow me one final go,' she said, hand on her heart which Meg couldn't resist. 'After which I promise to quit if it still doesn't work.'

'Go on then,' Meg laughed, knowing Esther too well, one of the finest people there was. She was goodness incarnate. Better than that; that rarest of beings, an honest politician.

'Please,' implored Esther, when she tracked him down. 'She treated you badly and always will but I can't just stand back and watch her destroy herself.'

Hugo twinkled. He'd matured a lot; life was treating him very well. Though still unmarried, he had many friends, a fair proportion of them female.

'Rose is her own worst enemy,' he said. 'Which each of us knows from experience. Though, due to her rarity of mind, I always allowed her to get away with murder.'

'But not any longer . . .'

'I'm afraid not,' he said. 'Life's too short to be kicked around. If I felt I could help, I would give it a shot. From what you say, she is on a downward spiral. But I'm too old now to go chasing hares. I lack both energy and incentive.'

He was right, of course. As she pedalled home, Esther thought sadly about poor Rose. Who, due to her meanness and self-obsession, was no longer cared about by anyone.

Not even Bunty, if truth be told, who was unceremoniously bundled off to a private home for special needs, with a clinic attached which meant she need never leave. Since Matthew died she had no protector except for the daughter who didn't care. Though she constantly asked where Lily was, nobody now had an answer.

'It's all right, dear. Here's a nice cup of tea. And why don't I plump up your cushions and turn on the telly? Supper's at five, it won't be long now. I don't know when Lily will come.'

The sale of the house meant clearing it out. Rose called in a reputable auctioneers which took the things of significant value but left her with the dross. Bitterly cursing beneath her breath, she drove out to Twick-enham at weekends to sort through the detritus of what had once been her family home. Where to start she had no idea. Bunty had lived in a welter of muddle with cupboards crammed with stuff long out of date. Rose's and Lily's baby shoes, lovingly wrapped in tissue paper and packed in boxes sprinkled with faded petals. Bunty's own wedding dress and veil with the elbow-length gloves, now yellowed with age, and the satin slippers she had only worn that one time.

Sackloads of clothes, carefully preserved for the daughters who'd not even tried them on. They might have been shipped to a costume museum had Rose remotely cared. To her, though, all they represented was the fashionable frippery she'd so much despised. She loaded the lot into her car and dropped it off at Oxfam.

Among her mother's more personal things, the satin slips and diaphanous nightgowns, she found a foolscap envelope, carefully sealed. She opened it with a kitchen knife, curious to see what it contained, and pulled out a handful of faded cuttings dating back thirty years. There she was, at six years old, smiling demurely into the camera while the mayor presented her with a bravery medal. The child who had pluckily risked her own life trying to rescue her infant brother.

A child in the spotlight for something she hadn't done.

50

Life returned to its regular tempo. Rose put her energies back into work. She had no excuse now not to get on with things. Convention said she should visit her mother though what was the point, she tried to explain, when minutes later Bunty no longer remembered she'd even been there? And, on the rare occasions she did, called her by Lily's name. They weren't too keen on Rose at the home. She was disagreeable when she was there as if they were somehow wasting her time by making her feel she should visit. Her mother's care was now up to them. Rose certainly paid enough to keep her there.

Later, seeking spiritual solace, she would sometimes drop into St John's, Smith Square and listen to music before she could face going home to an empty flat. Her favourite work was the St Matthew Passion, which spoke to her in ethereal ways, touching her soul mathematically along with its soaring message. She would close her eyes and sink into the music, translated to a higher plane where all the things that were gnawing at her miraculously faded away. Although not formally religious, she knew where to turn when she felt real pain and found some kind of absolution in the merging of her talents with something greater.

Later she'd enter her silent flat and stand awhile in the furry darkness, sensing an alien presence around her before she dared turn on the light. There was nothing there that was tangible yet, in those moments, she never felt more alone.

To start with he was a novelty, the baby brother she thought she wanted, a chubby smiling forerunner of Lily with dimples and fragrant skin. The image of his mother, they said, with sky blue eyes and the same wide smile. Too pretty for a boy, at least at that age. Four-year-old Rose took over his welfare, scooping him carefully out of his cot and carrying him, like an oversized toy, to lower him into his bath. Already she was a practical child and Bunty trusted her common sense. Soon she was bathing the baby alone with no older person there to supervise.

By five she was pushing him out in his pram, the envy of her neighbourhood friends who had no babies of their own, or none that they were allowed such freedom with. Simon was perpetually happy, a trusting contented biddable child who would crawl around on the grass at her feet in the spacious grounds of their parents' home, the riverside paradise built by their talented father.

'Keep him away from the water,' called Bunty, proud of her conscientious daughter.

'A proper little mother's helper,' cooed her friends.

At two, though, Simon became a pest, able to toddle and move at speed. Rose grew bored and irritated at constantly having to watch him. She couldn't go out now without him in tow and her friends preferred playing with makeup and dolls, though the mothers still paid full attention to the baby.

'You're really lucky she likes him so much. It is not unusual, at this age, for a bit of sibling rivalry to creep in.'

'Not with my Rose,' Bunty would brag. 'She is far too grown up for that sort of thing and will one day make a wonderful mother herself.'

Bunty played a good game of tennis; they had their own court at home to which she would often invite the lady members of her club. Before they had lunch they would play a few sets, nothing too strenuous, purely social, then loll around in the sunshine enjoying the views. Barges and cruisers would glide slowly by and Simon would chortle and leap up and down, drawing waves and blown kisses from the people aboard because he was so cute. Rose grew sour. It was not that long since she herself had got all the attention. She was tiring of Simon's chubby charms. Something would have to be done.

They were all at lunch when the incident happened. Bunty had never played tennis since. Nor would she ever sit facing the river again. When she heard the splash, Rose reported later, she jumped in beside him as fast as she could and tried to grab him under his arms though found him waterlogged and too heavy to hold. He went under twice before she screamed. By the time the mothers heard and came running, it was too late to revive him.

Later there was a formal inquiry and Rose was exonerated from blame. On the contrary, she had been very brave in trying to save her brother. Now, at night, when she couldn't sleep, she still remembered his staring eyes and the bubbles that came from his mouth as she forced him under.

Sukey's death had been more horrific. Again, it was the eyes Rose could not forget. Bleeding and sightless, they haunted her at the dead of night when she couldn't sleep, as disgusting now as they had been in life but deserved. The slut had been playing around with Joe, whether or not she'd admitted it, and had to be stopped before things went any further. As it turned out, it had served Rose well, though she still tried to block it from her mind. Five years had passed and the matter was closed. But she couldn't erase the image without a strong drink.

With shaking hands she would scramble some eggs which she then found she hadn't the stomach to eat so discarded in favour of whisky. Lily had been a thorn in her side, worse even than Simon by being a girl and coming along to fill his gap and assuage Bunty's terrible grief. At nine Rose was like a mini adult with her genius for maths and prowess at chess. Without meaning to, they had shut her out to concentrate on the baby. Lily, Rose had heard Bunty say, had been the fulfilment of a prayer and provided her with a reason for keeping on living. Lily, the saviour, had proved Rose's curse by snatching from her the one person she loved, thus consigning her to eternal torment and this bleakness of the soul. She, too, had to be sacrificed though this time not by her sister's hand. What she had got was her just deserts for which Rose felt no guilt.

On such nights she would switch off the light and try to sleep though usually she was too wired up to do more than doze. The whisky, which normally numbed her pain, had the converse effect. The darkness was filled with accusing eyes, all of them focused on her.

51

She was still wearing Lily's engagement ring though no longer bothered with manicures. Too expensive and frivolous, not the image of the woman she had become. She'd considered buying a wedding ring to endorse her newly revised persona then saw, in time, the scorn it would provoke in the department. Already they laughed behind her back; a ring could only make matters worse. She kept and framed Daisy's baby snaps and placed them, along with Joe's, on the bedside table. By rights they both belonged to her; still would if it weren't for greedy Annette who had hijacked them after Rose had disposed of Lily.

Which still gave her many sleepless nights. She often wondered what Joe was like now. In her dreams he had not altered at all, though in less than three years he'd be fifty. Occasionally he appeared in the news, on television addressing the UN, or chairing some international committee on the dangers of global warming. His hair seemed very much greyer now and the pouches beneath his eyes more pronounced, though the twisted sardonic smile appeared unaltered. Never exactly conventionally handsome, he had always been striking and debonair with a dangerous glint in his eye most women found thrilling. All age had done was add to his bearing. Rose's endless longing intensified.

She went to concerts on her own, avoiding the eyes of those around her. The last thing she wanted to be was picked up though she did feel wistful whenever she heard others laughing. She studied the score in the interval and read the programme from cover to cover. To bring a book would look too pathetic, she felt. Later she'd stroll home through the crowds to her empty flat with its deathly silence and prepare herself a frugal meal to eat on her knee in front of the late night news. What sort of life was this? she wondered, but couldn't devise any way to improve her lot.

There was no one at work in whom to confide. They looked upon her as a kind of pariah. Too much power and too short a fuse. Not one to be trusted. She sat alone in her office each day where only the very bravest dared disturb her. Even Esther only rarely phoned and usually, when she did, it was just to check in. Her diary, these days, seemed perpetually full. Rose blamed their estrangement on Meg.

Statistics were not exactly exciting though from them Rose drew a quiet satisfaction. Provided she could complete her tables and throw some light on the country's woes, she cleared her desk at the end of each day with a feeling of achievement. It calmed and soothed her to do this work from which she could draw a conclusive answer. If the columns balanced the world was not in such bad array after all.

She was seated alone at the Festival Hall, reading the paper one dismal Sunday, waiting to hear Strauss's Oboe Concerto which was only rarely performed these days, when she heard distinctly, close by, a voice she knew. She glanced up quickly and there was Hugo, talking rapidly into his phone just a couple of tables away. At first he looked blank when she waved to him, then his face broke into the old, sweet smile.

'Rose, how nice to see you,' he said, gathering his things and moving across to join her.

He was looking good and her pulse raced though she now wished she'd made an effort herself. She was out of the habit of dressing up, no longer even bothered to do her face. But this was Hugo, her long-time swain who had never concealed his infatuation. She gave him a hug and he pecked her cheek, then dumped his papers and scarf on a chair.

'Are you on your own?' And when she said yes, went to the bar to fetch them both glasses of wine.

'Long time no see.' He seemed very relaxed though Rose remembered the lie she had told. It must be almost five years; how fast time went. She wished she wasn't wearing the ring and hoped that he wouldn't comment on it. If he did she would tell the truth, that it was Lily's.

'So,' he said. 'What have you been up to? Are you still running the DTI?'

She laughed. 'Well, not quite running,' she said, looking bashful.

He was more relaxed, as Esther had said. His hair was sleek and he was well groomed. He no longer wore the old beat-up brogues, was even sporting a tie. She asked about his publishing job and he came alight, as he always had when anyone showed any interest in his work. He talked about the authors he published and revealed that he, too, was writing a book.

'Nothing very ambitious,' he said, 'but it fills a gap in the list.'

She cautiously asked if he still performed but he shook his head and his smile went away. After a fairly discernible pause, he told her he'd given up when she'd ended their friendship.

Rose felt awkward, had nothing to add. Now was the moment she ought to come clean. But Esther had said she'd run into him and so he undoubtedly knew. They sat in silence; she checked the time. Still twenty minutes till the performance. She badly wanted to put things right, to ask forgiveness and maybe start again. This was Hugo; apart from Esther her closest and most durable friend. What a fool she had been; she could see it now and hoped it wasn't too late to make amends.

She cleared her throat. She would take the plunge and throw herself on to his infinite kindness. He had always been such a loyal friend and would surely not desert her now. But Hugo had pushed his chair away, was up on his feet and frantically waving.

'Over here!' he yelled to someone faceless in the crowd.

The girl who approached looked calm and poised, with straight fair hair and a radiant smile. It was clear from Hugo's body language that this was more than just a casual friend. He turned to introduce her to Rose who said she really had to go. She wanted to pick up a programme before they went in.

She left the hall and went straight home, no longer in the mood for music. Even Hugo had now moved on. It seemed that everyone in the world had someone else in their life apart from her.

52

She wasn't expecting the Christmas card. It dropped through the door with a handful of bills and there was Daisy, now almost six, cheerfully smiling and clutching a couple of kittens. *Thinking of you*, Annette had scrawled. *Daisy is doing well at school, especially in maths and physics. Must take after you!*

She did, indeed, have a slight look of Rose with her narrow eyes and neatly bobbed hair. Joe had also signed his name which intensified the anguish. After the first sharp impact of shock, Rose seized up, her face white with rage, her fingers trembling as she ripped up the card and hurled the pieces in the bin. How dare that woman flaunt Lily's child, the niece she wasn't allowed to see. After a while, she fished out the card and carefully taped it together.

Christmas promised to be grisly this year, with Matthew dead and Bunty still on the decline. She would visit the home in the afternoon but not stay long; there was little point. She hated her mother's blank expression and the fact that she persisted in thinking she was Lily. Other than that she had no fixed plans, except perhaps Midnight Mass in the cathedral. The soaring music calmed her soul and helped her forget how alone she was. After that she would go to ground for the rest of the holiday break. The flat looked dreary, with no Christmas lights and only a handful of formal cards sent by various notables in the department. None from Esther, who was not of the faith, nor from Hugo which equally hurt. She'd not heard a word from him since that wretched last meeting.

Her thoughts went back to her happy childhood and the Christmases then that had meant so much. Their home had reverberated with laughter the whole of the festive season. Bunty had cooked and Lily shown off and the beautiful house had come into its own, swathed with holly and mistletoe and crowned by the splendid tree. The neighbours came in every Boxing Day and invited them back for New Year's Eve. Though non-believers, they went to church to join in the spirit of things. Even Matthew had put down his paper, poured the sherry and carved the bird and helped pull crackers like any regular dad.

The flat felt chilly and even dank but it might just

be the contrast she felt. On the run up to Christmas the shops stayed open every night of the week. Rose bought slippers for Bunty and chocolates for the nurses but otherwise had no presents to give. She donated fifty pounds to the department towards mince pies and champagne.

'Won't you come and join us?' they asked, popping their heads round her office door.

'Start without me,' she said. 'I have work to complete.'

The thought of them shrieking and larking around was too much for her with her delicate nerves. Once she'd cleared her desk she would slip away and treat herself to some finest quality Scotch.

At this time of year the flat was depressing with no morning sunshine to warm it up. The electric fire was a dismal failure and the central light in the living room had a single bulb with a dark green shade that failed to do its job. She really needed a reading lamp, had a constant headache from having to squint, but since she lacked all domestic skills she hadn't the vaguest idea how to make a place cosy. Bunty possessed that talent in spades. Rose wished now she had been an attentive daughter.

The Markovich card stood on the shelf, flanked by the only two jolly ones: from the newsagent's boy, soliciting alms, and also a neighbourhood Indian restaurant in which she had never set foot. Rose endlessly studied the picture of Daisy, clumsily mended but still clear enough, searching her face for signs of her heritage. She was not like Lily, more like herself, but in this snap Rose could find no trace of Joe. Which, in a way, was comforting. She was so possessive, she could not have borne anyone's too obviously sharing his blood.

They were singing carols in the street below. She hoped they wouldn't ring her bell and expect her to give them money. She hated Christmas more each year. It took her back to that fatal night when Joe came to pick her up at home and caught her mother and sister decking the tree. Lily, with tinsel in her hair, acting the fool and showing off. If Joe hadn't grabbed her as she fell he wouldn't even have noticed her and life might have taken the path that destiny intended.

She was restless now and also chilly. This flat that was hers didn't feel like home. She decided to go for a walk to warm herself up. She passed the carollers but didn't stop, in no way touched by the spirit of Christmas which was really no more than the winter solstice, the darkest and dreariest days of the year. The rain had ceased and the air was fresh. Her head was aching from too much Scotch.

Suddenly she was in Pimlico, facing the doorway

of Joe's block. She couldn't resist a quick peek inside at the glorious welcoming tree.

'Hello there.' The porter remembered her and came out, rubbing his hands, for a chat. How was she faring, he asked, and how was the baby?

Both of them well, Rose told him brightly. Daisy was six now and at school.

His kind eyes twinkled like Santa Claus. 'You must bring her round to see me,' he said. 'Though there's no way she would remember me. She was only a few months old when they moved out.'

Rose said she would then hurried away before he could start to reminisce, steeped in even further gloom by this ever painful reminder of what she had lost. It had only ever been fantasy. Annette had annexed the pair of them before Rose's love and Joe's had had time to take root. Her spirits darkened; she ought not be here. If only Jean-Paul had not died. If only they'd never met at all. If Joe had not returned to the States he would still be here with her where he belonged.

It drizzled all the way down to the home, putting her into an even worse mood. Most other inmates had family there; only Bunty was sitting alone with a foolish satin bow in her hair and her cheeks all rouged like a garish Victorian doll. Rose handed her the neatly wrapped package and watched as she marvelled at the slippers. She had an identical pair every year but managed to get through them. The nurses hinted at incontinence which was more information than Rose could bear. The details of her mother's decline were too horrendous to face up to.

'Is Lily coming?' The chant never changed, those innocent eyes roving round the room in the hope of a glimpse of the daughter she'd so much adored.

'Not today.' Rose was weary already and still had to face the long drive home. Soon, at four, they'd be serving lunch and then she could slip away. Bunty was perfectly happy here, would not even notice that she had gone. She wondered why she had come at all. Then remembered it was Christmas.

The night seemed darker; it was raining still and Rose's hands were chilled to the bone. She longed to sit by a blazing fire and make herself a hot toddy. She climbed the stairs in her silent block and let herself into the empty flat. The forty-watt bulb blew out with a bang and left her alone in the darkness with her demons.

53

It was Esther who actually let it slip though, had she thought, she must have known what damage it could do. Joe was coming over in March to speak about global warming at a Royal Society conference. Feverishly Rose checked out the date. She had nothing special at all that week but time, she hoped, to work a transition on her looks. She booked the hairdresser for her roots and tried to cut down on her liquor consumption. Put out to grass the old lady shoes and resurrected the heels for which she'd been known. Let them laugh at her in the office; she no longer cared. All that mattered to her, as always, was Joe.

He would be in London. Another chance. This time she hadn't got room for error. One final throw of the dice; she had to win. After careful thought, she wrote to Annette, saying she'd heard Joe would be in town and asking if she was coming too and possibly bringing

Daisy. A lengthy pause then Annette replied. Daisy, alas, had to be in school but she would be coming herself; they would certainly meet.

Rose felt dizzy. It had been five years. She must reconstruct the way she had been and not allow her consuming hatred to show. Somehow, whatever it took, she would win this round.

Since they'd be staying at the Savoy, Rose dropped by on the false pretence that she was someone's PA. She wanted to check out the suites, she said, and made up some story about a client. She didn't know what she was looking for though would know it when she found it. The suites they showed her were of various sizes, some of them with a river view, decorated in traditional style with state of the art technology controlled by touch pads and sensors. Rose was thrilled. It was just the job. Something for her to work on

'Thanks,' she said, presenting her card, one she had filched from a colleague's desk. 'I'll be in touch,' she promised, 'nearer the time.'

The Royal Society was very prestigious and Joe would be one of the principal speakers. The conference would last for three days. She didn't know if he would be there all the time.

She wrote again, full of friendly chat, to cement the cracks in their erstwhile friendship, updating Annette on the poor state of Bunty's health. It was doubly sad Daisy couldn't come too. Perhaps she could visit them in the summer to spend some quality time with her gran. She mentioned Lily's engagement ring, though not that she had been wearing it. She said her sister would have wanted her daughter to have it.

Annette, who had not been aware of the ring, answered that it was generous of Rose. For security's sake, she would pick it up when they met. So the die was cast; there was no going back. All Rose had to come up with now was the actual scene of the crime and, of course, the method. She had murdered twice; it was no big deal. Provided her plan was feasible and foolproof.

She threw herself into a frenzied routine of exercise, diet and ruthless reinvention. In the past few years she had let herself go; by now it was starting to show. Out went the frumpish mid-calf skirts and the cardigans she had taken to wearing. Back came the snappy knee-length suits and crisp well-laundered blouses. If anyone noticed, they didn't say though she guessed they were talking behind closed doors. Her passion for Joe had been widely observed and the whole world knew what had happened to her sister. She deserved a second chance, some felt, though most just found her annoying and absurd.

She decided also to spruce up the flat. She'd done little to it since moving in and, because of her paranoia, had not even hired a cleaner. Now and again she dusted a bit and pushed the Hoover round on Sunday mornings. Mostly, though, she was so self-absorbed she was barely even aware of her surroundings. But things were changing; the light grew brighter. Soon it would be spring. She saw how smeared the windows were and how grubby everything was. She hauled down the curtains Bunty had made and sent them off to be properly cleaned. She shook up the cushions and straightened the rug, even polished the few bits of silver she'd kept when she sold the Twickenham house.

She brushed up on her culinary skills; had let it all slide when Joe went away. Bought new china and had the cooker serviced. She was acting like a foolish girl, which showed in the glass when she looked at herself. Her skin was flushed, her eyes were bright. Her hormones had come out of hibernation. She started listening to jazz again, and even hip-hopped round the room, flapping her duster and swinging her hips as she sought to bring back meaning to her life.

They were staying a week which was not much time. She was sure they would have other people to see. Joe was coming as an emissary, not on vacation. She would have to get Annette on her own, perhaps take her on a shopping spree. Though Annette was not the kind of woman to care about such things. A matinee would be far more up her street. As time grew shorter, Rose grew tense. She might never get such a chance again. She racked her brains for methods of killing and bought some expensive lingerie just in case.

She also bought a couple of lamps to improve the light in her living room as well as a sofa in the January sales. Atmosphere was important, she'd read. She wanted to make them feel at home, assuming they would allow her to entertain them. But she was family, no escaping that, aunt to the only child they had. She must have some legal rights, though couldn't be certain. The important thing was to get them here and subtly work her way into their trust. The rest would follow; of that she was confident.

The room looked good once she'd moved things about and shoved the armchairs apart to make space for the sofa. The reading lamps made all the difference, providing a glow that enhanced the room. She remembered Christmas, when the sole bulb had blown, plunging her into sudden darkness.

Which was when inspiration struck. And she knew exactly how she was going to do it.

54

Physics was not Rose's greatest strength, though her grasp of mathematics made things that much clearer. Her Joe fixation had also helped by making her more conversant with the subject. She'd had open access to his papers on the occasions he was away and had spent a large proportion of the time in his study, quietly browsing. Now an hour in the library sufficed before moving on to the internet. The basic mechanics should not prove too hard, provided she could manage the fiddly part. It might take practice to get it perfect but she still had a few weeks in hand. The vital thing was to get it right. She didn't intend to bungle or get caught.

The important thing was to visit the suite and adapt her device to whatever was there. The ones she had seen all had vestibules, the ideal situation for her ersatz bomb. The size of the light fitting mattered too. The larger the better for her purposes. It would take a massive explosion to kill so she needed it to be confined.

She wrote to Annette and also to Daisy, restoring herself, she hoped, in their eyes as the generous maiden aunt she aspired to be. To make up for her recent neglect, she hoped to spend as much time with Annette as she could. She had Lily's ring professionally cleaned and repackaged in a satin-lined box. She regretted having to give it up but now had a far more compelling aim. From now on all or nothing was her mantra.

March approached and her plan was complete. At first she considered a trial run then rejected that as being far too risky. As with the other murders she'd committed, she would only get a single shot which meant every detail had to be right, even if not rehearsed.

They'd arrive on a Sunday, were staying a week. Joe's big moment was on Thursday at three though he'd be at the conference also on Tuesday and Wednesday. On Friday they planned a visit to Oxford; on Saturday lunchtime they would leave. Rose, who thrived on organisation, was glad to get hold of the chapter and verse. It gave her a little leeway to play with though hardly any space for a last minute change. She invited them to come for a meal but Annette insisted she dine with them. Joe had a lot on his mind right now; she knew Rose would understand. Rose was pleased; things were working out precisely as she had hoped they might. Annette was playing right into her hands.

She had her biannual lunch with Esther.

'You're at it again,' Esther said. She could tell from the glint in Rose's eye (she was back to wearing her contacts again) that something was going on that she wasn't telling. All of a sudden she'd come alive and had shed the signs of ageing she'd shown. Her hair was glossy, her skin was clear. She hadn't looked this good in years, not since before Joe remarried.

'What's going on?' Esther knew her too well not to suspect her motivation. Whenever Rose was this lit up, it invariably boded no good.

'Nothing,' said Rose with an innocent smile. The past, she explained, was now well behind her. She was looking forward to seeing Joe and hearing all about Daisy. 'He is my brother-in-law,' she said. 'Allow me some family ties.'

'Yeah,' said Esther cynically, once more quietly despairing inside. Meg was right; this woman was evil. 'Pull the other one.'

'I'm really fond of Annette,' said Rose which, to start with, had been the truth. Though circumstances had intervened, they had once got on very well. Now she was hoping to put behind her the hostility caused by this second marriage. Annette was married to Daisy's father; that was as far as it went.

'Please be happy for me,' she implored. 'I am doing all I can to make amends.'

She laid out her tools on the kitchen table having first made sure that the blinds were down. She didn't want anyone seeing what she was up to. The diagram, which she had enhanced, dated back more than two hundred years. Science since then had come on immeasurably and yet the basic device still worked though, these days, in a far more complex form. Now *that* was genius; Rose was impressed as she studied the basic simplicity that had revolutionised the world perhaps even more than the wheel. From everyday commodities purchased from a hardware store she was able to magnify the power of this run-of-the-mill device. She turned it over in her hands, admiring its smooth simplicity. She understood the physics of it; now all she needed was the expertise and sleight of hand to alter it enough to make it effective. With tweezers and a steady hand she needed to fill the orb with gas derived from acetylene of which she already had a sufficient supply. Thank goodness for vanity, she grinned, and the fact that, due to Joe's return, she was painting her nails again.

If this didn't work, she would try again until she

was certain it couldn't go wrong. Fingerprints were not an issue. If it did work, there wouldn't be anything left behind.

'Do you mind coming here?' asked Annette when she called. 'Joe's got a meeting all afternoon so we thought we'd eat in the Grill.'

'That's fine with me,' said Rose. It was part of her plan. She had only once dined in the hotel but had been back lately a couple of times to have a solitary drink in the bar and suss out the general layout.

'See you at eight, then.' Annette sounded cheery. Rose made an effort to bite back her hatred and answer in similar vein.

She arrived deliberately seven minutes early and called the room from the crowded lobby.

'Goodness,' Annette said, 'do you mind coming up? Joe is only just back from his meeting.'

'My fault,' said Rose. 'I'm a little early. I had a clear ride through.' It suited her to go upstairs. She needed to inspect the scene of the crime. There were little details she had to check to make her plan go faultlessly. She wouldn't, after all, get another chance.

Their suite was on the second floor, three doors along from the lift. Rose rapidly combed her hair and checked her lipstick. She wore a narrow navy coat dress that stopped abruptly at the knee, with three-inch heels that added to her stature. She had almost worn the Garbo hat but that, she decided, would be in poor taste. No reminders of Lily tonight, not in the circumstances.

Annette looked good when she opened the door, unchanged since the last time they'd met. Her smile was as wide and unfeigned as before and the hug she gave Rose seemed sincere.

'My, you're looking chic,' she said. 'I'm afraid I am travelling very light.' She didn't have a hair out of place, was her usual soignée self. She led the way through the vestibule, with its black Murano glass chandelier, so large that even Rose had to duck for fear of knocking her head. Exactly right for her purposes; she couldn't have planned it better. Low enough for her to reach and the black Venetian glass would conceal the bomb.

'I like the mix of tradition and modern.' She had also noticed the lighting sensors.

Annette agreed. 'They have done us proud. And given us one of the better suites. Guess that's because Joe's now a VIP.'

'I particularly like the chandelier.'

'Isn't it great? Like being in Venice. Joe's in the shower. He's only just back. I've ordered wine. I hope that's OK with you.'

Rose strolled over to look at the view, one of the

most famous in London, then turned and surveyed the room at large, approving of what she saw. Joe had come a long way up in the world; well, she supposed they all had. The outfit she wore was Prada, the shoes Jimmy Choo. A waiter tapped and brought in a tray which he set on the table in front of the fire.

'Just pour for two,' Annette directed. 'My husband's not yet ready.'

'Wrong,' said a voice and there he stood, knotting his tie in the bedroom doorway. Rose's heart gave a mighty lurch as she slowly turned and came face to face with Joe.

55

Words could not describe how she felt. Despite the months of anticipation, she was still unprepared for the frisson of shock when she saw him in the flesh. Gaunt and drawn, though very distinguished, with the famous pouchy eyes and sardonic smile. His hair was still thick though now very much greyer, and beneath the well-cut suit he looked in good shape. He held out his hands, one by one, to his wife and, after she had fastened his cufflinks, leaned across and pecked Rose on both cheeks.

'You look well,' he said, as if he cared. 'Are you still with the DTI?'

Rose nodded, already inwardly choking. There wasn't a thing about him she didn't know. These days he was constantly in the news, an eminence in his chosen field often brought in to pontificate on crises affecting the world. She remembered her father's prophecy, that his government job would lead to a knighthood. By now, had he stayed, he would doubtless have been ennobled. And Annette would be Lady Markovich. She remembered Lily's excited posing and something inside her curled up and died. The jealousy was still there. Which reminded her, or so she said.

'Damn, I've forgotten Lily's ring. Which means,' she added with a wide fake smile, 'we will have to meet up again.'

Dinner was lively. They made a good team and appeared, Rose had to admit, well matched. Most of the time Joe held the floor while Annette always gave him her utmost attention, hanging on to his words with her gentle smile. She clearly adored him; that much was plain, but then she had also adored Jean-Paul. Rose bit down on her bitterness. What sort of woman could she be, who could love like that more than once? Despite her beauty, which was classic and lasting, Annette was extremely intelligent too and had only stopped working full time when she married Joe.

'Daisy needed a lot of loving, especially after what they'd been through. Although she doesn't remember her mother, we do what we can to keep her memory alive.'

Hence the ring. It was a generous gesture. Joe looked

blank when Annette brought it up again. Rose held her breath in case he asked questions but so much had happened since Lily's death he had clearly never given it a thought. She still had the jewellery she'd stowed away which now, she reckoned, she need not return. Annette was wearing diamonds that outranked Lily's.

She seethed inside. It was so unfair. That ring, by rights, should be on her own finger. She could have raised her sister's child as her own, and many more.

It was like the night with Annette and Jean-Paul. When the evening ended they called for a cab and left her to fend for herself. Gone were the days when Joe himself would valiantly flag one down in the street and wait until she was safely in before he trotted back home. She had seen the private looks they'd exchanged, the knowledge that she would soon be gone; that this formal evening would finally end and they could be together. She knew the feeling. It had haunted her dreams almost every night since she'd first seen Joe. Twenty-three years ago in Rick's Bar. Half a lifetime.

'Thank you so much.' She hugged them both and told them to go back up to the suite. The desk would tell her when the cab arrived. Tomorrow would be a heavy one for Joe. She arranged with Annette to drop off the ring. Would call beforehand to check she was there. 'I will bring it up to the room,' she joked. 'We can't have you being mugged.'

'Nice evening?' the driver casually inquired, in that condescending way they had as if a woman alone was easy prey.

'Mind your own damn business. Just drive,' said Rose.

She kicked off her shoes and poured a Scotch, then threw herself on to the sofa, weeping. The hatred she'd kept buttoned up inside overflowed. He belonged to her and always had. Just being with him drove her out of her mind, especially when he seemed hardly aware she was there. The way that woman had primped and fawned, fluttered her eyelashes shamelessly as if to keep him away from her. Well, that was hardly surprising. She blew her nose and splashed her face, then refilled her glass with a shaking hand. Even Annette must have been aware how much they were in tune.

From the very first time she had heard him play she had known their lives were for ever entwined. Greater powers than theirs had brought them together. Lily had flirted then snatched him away but little good had come of that. Her early death and an unforeseen child that had also hastened the sharp decline of her parents. If things had taken their natural course, she would be Lady Markovich now, Lily would still be alive and so would Matthew. Bunty would not be stuck in that home, thinking each stranger was back from the dead. Daisy would not exist at all, having never been born.

Rose and Joe would have their own brood and live somewhere gracious, like the outskirts of Oxford, where by now he would be a full professor. Their children would all be musically gifted and on Sunday nights, by a blazing fire, would join him round the piano for a sing-song. She would accompany them on the flute and Hugo would still be a valued friend. Godfather to one of them; of course, he would never have married. Even Esther would still be around . . . At which point Rose began weeping again. If only Annette had not come on the scene just when she had things under control with Sukey disposed of and Lily out of the picture. Annette was the cause of her misery now. She had stolen Joe and was raising Daisy. Things could not be allowed to happen this way.

She hurled her Waterford glass at the wall where it shattered like a miniature bomb.

'Die, bitch, die!' she screamed in unhinged fury.

56

On Thursday Joe was speaking at three. Annette would join him later for the reception.

'He hates me being there at these things, though it's hard to believe I could make him nervous.' Joe was a seasoned speaker now after so many years on the circuit. Annette sounded happy, not to say smug, as well she might for she had it all. Rose gritted her teeth and tried to force some gaiety into her voice.

'I thought I'd drop by around lunchtime,' she said. 'I finally remembered Lily's ring. But if you're busy, I could leave it at the desk . . .'

'No, bring it up to the suite,' said Annette. 'You can't be too careful with these things.' Then, clearly aware that she sounded brusque, she insisted that Rose stay for lunch. 'I don't have very much time,' she explained. 'I'm having my hair done at quarter to three, the only slot the salon could fit me into.'

'Well, if you're sure.' It was perfectly timed. She could make it back to work within half an hour. No one need know she had even been out; she spent so much time in her office alone, the door firmly closed as she ate a solitary sandwich. 'If you like, I could always bring something in.'

'Of course not,' replied Annette, appalled. 'I'll call room service. Would a salad do? It's what I usually have.'

'Perfect,' said Rose. 'I'll be there soon after one.'

Which should allow her just enough time. She assumed Annette would want to shower before going up to the salon for her hairdo. She opened the box and took out the ring, slipping it on to her finger again. She regretted having to give it up though it might survive the blast. Daisy need never know what she'd lost; she would make it up to her in other ways.

Today, because the wind was sharp, she did, indeed, wear the Garbo hat. Not only did it add dignity but it would double as a disguise. No one would notice her in that crowd; the lobby of the Savoy was always swarming. And Joe would be long gone at his morning session. Once she was ready she took out the bomb, solidly packing it all round with cotton wool before wrapping it carefully in kitchen foil. This was the trickiest part of all; she couldn't risk breaking it in her bag even though, without the fuse, it wouldn't go off. But the slightest jolt could destroy her hard work and abort the delicate mission. All things considered, she opted for taking a cab.

'It's me,' she said on the lobby phone.

'Come up,' said Annette. 'I'm doing my nails.'

The door was open so Rose walked in. The light went on in the lobby.

'I love this modern technology.' She tossed her hat on the nearest chair but clung to her bag which she didn't want to let go of.

'Isn't it great? It's the same throughout. Walk anywhere and the lights come on. And after midnight they dim themselves, presumably not to wake you. And if you take a nocturnal stroll, Joe tells me they follow discreetly. I confess I could get addicted to this lifestyle.'

There were speakers, too, in every room, concealed in all the salient points. Wherever you went, the music flowed. Annette was playing an Erik Satie CD.

'One of Joe's,' she explained to Rose. 'It helps to calm him down.'

'I'd have thought by now he'd be used to it.' Rose hated it when she mentioned Joe as if she knew him better than she did which, after five years of marriage, perhaps she did.

'Today's a big occasion,' said Annette. 'Most of the

world will be looking in. He can't afford to make a fool of himself.'

'As if,' said Rose with a grin. Then lunch arrived.

It was more relaxed than she'd dared to hope. Annette seemed in tremendous form and had Rose chuckling over the lobster salad.

'You must come and stay with us,' she said. 'And get to know your clever niece. The more she grows, the more like you she becomes.'

'I'd like that,' said Rose with a twinge of regret, steeling herself for the job in hand. 'Hadn't you better start getting ready? I'll just finish my wine, if you don't mind, and then I'll slip away.'

'You're right,' said Annette. It was two fifteen. 'I need to shower before I dress.'

She left and Rose strolled over to the window.

The second she heard the water start, Rose returned to the vestibule. The light came on. She found the touchpad, touched it and it went off again, she assumed deactivated. Very gently she opened her bag and extracted the delicate foil-wrapped package. One false move could trigger the whole thing off. With meticulous care, she unscrewed a bulb, replacing it with the bomb she'd made, positioning it where it wouldn't show though nobody would be checking. The lightest touch on the sensor pad would switch it over to automatic, leaving her just sixty seconds to get clear.

The sound of the shower abruptly ceased; time for Rose to be leaving fast. As soon as Annette was dressed she'd be off for her hairdo.

She considered the stairs; it was just two floors, but the lift had arrived. And Joe stepped out.

'What on earth?' she gasped but he didn't hear, hardly noticed her, was clearly preoccupied. She stood in his way to block his path but he pushed straight past without slowing his pace.

'I forgot my reading glasses,' he said. 'Can't be late, I am on at three. The driver's illegally parked.'

She tried to stop him by clutching his sleeve. It wasn't supposed to end like this. But Joe was practically at the door.

She fled like a terrified rabbit.

57

The sharp explosion rocked the place. Rose just made it to the lobby though no one even noticed her. It was, as usual, packed. The concierge, startled by the bang, took his master keys off the board and started off up the stairs to investigate. She couldn't bear not to wait and see though common sense urged her to run for it. Whatever had happened to Joe she would find out later.

It had started to rain which suited her well as it camouflaged her blinding tears as she crossed the road and headed along the Strand. She couldn't believe it had gone so wrong after all her painstaking preparations. She prayed that something had happened to save his life. She was into the Mall when she heard the sirens and a posse of police cars swept by. She hoped it might be royalty but her heart told her it was not.

Where she went after that she did not recall, just walked and wept in the driving rain, glad of the hat that shielded her eyes and gave her some privacy. No way could she go back to work but nor could she face that silent flat. She knew from now on she was on her own unless a miracle happened.

At five she hopped on a 52 bus, too tired and cold to keep on walking, and saw from the top stark confirmation of all her wildest fears.

World Famous Scientist Blown Up. Terrorist Fears at Conference. She didn't need to buy the paper to find out what had happened.

They had been together, what was left of them, in the vestibule of their hotel suite. Most of the room had been wrecked by a bomb primed to go off when anyone passed the sensor. Whoever did it was fearless or mad, perhaps a combination of both. It was assumed Joe had been the target because of his world-saving mission. There followed columns of stuff about him, praising his work and great eminence. He was killed with his second wife, it said. Survived by his only child.

58

She came down the steps of the aeroplane, a small neat figure in a baseball cap, carrying her worldly goods in a duffel bag. Glancing neither to right or left, she followed the crowd into Passport Control and thence to the Arrivals Lounge where she'd been told she'd be met.

Rose, in black from head to foot, the way she would dress for the rest of her life, saw her and knew instinctively who she was.

'Daisy?'

'Aunt Rose.' She was self-possessed and displayed no emotion at being there. Clung to her bag and would not allow Rose to take it.

'Good flight?'

'All right. What happens now?'

'I thought perhaps you might like some lunch.'

The child shook her head. She was six years old, facing her sole surviving relative.

'I had some food on the plane,' she said. 'Let's go home.'

Home. What she meant was Rose's flat, tidied in haste to make room for her. For now she would live in the tiny spare room till Rose figured out what to do. Not being a naturally tactile person, she didn't know what was expected of her, but the child had lost both parents and must be in shock. She reached out with a tentative hand which Daisy ignored as she followed her. None of that sentimental stuff was her message.

Electrified, Rose knew she'd met her match, was face to face with her natural heir. She looked in those coolly appraising eyes.

And recognised herself.

KENSINGTON COURT

Carol Smith

In flight from a violent relationship, Kate Ashenberry arrives in London and find sanctuary in a vast Victorian mansion block which will, she hopes, give her the anonymity and security she seeks. Disillusioned by her lover and abandoned by her family, she faces the prospect of Christmas alone with only a stray kitten for company. Gradually, however, she gets to know her new neighbours; the daffy, delightful Barclay-Davenports next door; the exotic Eleni across the hall with her secret life; high-flying Miles with his chilly, ambitious wife; aristocratic Lady Wentworth whose family made her a Lloyds name; charming, uncatchable Gregory Hansen; and the awful Mrs Adelaide Potter, who dominates the other residents with her ruthless autocracy and acid tongue. And lovely Connie Boyle, the New York actress who becomes Kate's best friend.

As their lives grow closer and begin to merge, Kate discovers she has a whole new family. And yet something is not quite right. Some of the residents seem almost too friendly and occasionally, Kate feels she is being watched. It is only when the killing starts that the cosy camaraderie of Kensington Court collapses entirely. For no one, not even Kate, can foresee who the friendly neighbour will pick as the next victim.

DOUBLE EXPOSURE

Carol Smith

Joanna Lyndhurst is taking a well-earned break on the island of Antigua – ten days of sunshine, without anyone knowing she's a doctor. But Jo is not the only one concealing the truth. Amongst the enchanting and diverse bunch of characters she meets, it turns out not one is quite what they seem.

Lowell and Vincent have travelled the world in a long-standing relationship, while maintaining separate lives and private worlds that do not overlap. New York banking executive, Merrily, amuses them with her tales of Manhattan high-life yet conceals her real anxiety about the threat to her own career. Jessica, steeped in an world of culture and classical music, mourns a lost love whom she dare not discuss. And Cora Louise and Fontaine, mother and daughter from the steamy South, intent on hiding their own murky secret. The holiday becomes an annual tradition as close friendships develop and the group starts to meet on each others' home ground. Yet the Caribbean sunshine has its own darker side. Someone is on the trail of a killer . . .

'A good escapist read'
Express on Sunday

'An unusual and exciting yarn . . . a hugely enjoyable book'
Woman and Home

Other bestselling titles available by mail:

☐	Darkening Echoes	Carol Smith	£6.99
☐	Kensington Court	Carol Smith	£6.99
☐	Double Exposure	Carol Smith	£6.99
☐	Unfinished Business	Carol Smith	£6.99
☐	Grandmother's Footsteps	Carol Smith	£5.99
☐	Home from Home	Carol Smith	£5.99
☐	Hidden Agenda	Carol Smith	£6.99
☐	Vanishing Point	Carol Smith	£6.99
☐	Without Warning	Carol Smith	£6.99

The prices shown above are correct at time of going to press. However, the publishers reserve the right to increase prices on covers from those previously advertised without prior notice.

─────────────── sphere ───────────────

SPHERE
PO Box 121, Kettering, Northants NN14 4ZQ
Tel: 01832 737525, Fax: 01832 733076
Email: aspenhouse@FSBDial.co.uk

POST AND PACKING:

Payments can be made as follows: cheque, postal order (payable to Sphere), credit card or Maestro. Do not send cash or currency.

All UK Orders	**FREE OF CHARGE**
EC & Overseas	25% of order value

Name (BLOCK LETTERS) . . . .

Address . . . .

. . . .

Post/zip code: . . . .

☐ Please keep me in touch with future Sphere publications

☐ I enclose my remittance £ . . . .

☐ I wish to pay by Visa/Mastercard/Eurocard/Maestro

Card Expiry Date ☐☐☐☐   Maestro Issue No. ☐☐